DEATH

of an
Honourable
Gent

Eliza Thomson Investigates

Book 3

By

VL McBeath

Death of an Honourable Gent
By VL McBeath

For more about this author please visit:
https://vlmcbeath.com

*

Editing services provided by Susan Cunningham (www.
perfectproseservices.com)
Cover design by Michelle Abrahall (www.michelleabrahall.com)

ISBNs:

978-1-9999426-8-7 (Kindle Edition)
978-1-9999426-9-4 (Paperback)

Main category - FICTION / Historical Mysteries
Other category - FICTION / Crime & Mystery

CAST OF CHARACTERS

Eliza Thomson: Doctor's wife and amateur sleuth
Dr Archie Thomson: Eliza's husband
Henry Thomson: The son of Eliza and Dr Thomson
Mr Bell: Eliza's father
Mrs Connie Appleton: Eliza's friend and next-door
neighbour

The Aristocracy

Lord Lowton (Neville): Earl of Lowton
Lady Caroline Lowton: Lord Lowton's wife
Lord Albert Lowton: The son of Lord Lowton and Lady
Caroline
Lady Alice Lowton: The daughter of Lord Lowton and Lady
Caroline
Lady Hilda Forsyth: Lord Lowton's sister
Lord Forsyth: Lady Hilda's husband
The Honourable (Sir) Cyril Lowton: Lord Lowton's brother
Lady Victoria Lowton: Sir Cyril's wife
Lord David Lowton: The son of Sir Cyril and Lady Victoria
Lady Mary Lowton: The daughter of Sir Cyril and Lady
Victoria
Sir Rodney Brough: Lady Caroline's father
Lady Rosemary Brough: Lady Caroline's mother
Lord Beaufort: Family friend and lawyer
Lady Beaufort: Lord Beaufort's wife

Soams: The butler

Colonel Hawkins: The estate manager

Inspector Adams: Police inspector from New Scotland Yard

CHAPTER ONE

Eliza Thomson tossed the invitation onto the dining table and plonked her hands on her hips.

"What do you mean you can't go? You've known about this weekend for months."

Archie sighed and looked up from his breakfast. "I know, but I can't leave the village without a doctor, not now Dr Wark can't cover for me."

"I thought you'd arranged it with him."

"I had, but I got a letter from him this morning to say that he has to go away on a private matter."

Eliza closed her eyes and paced to the other side of the room. "Why can he go away and you can't? Did he even ask you?" Eliza stared at her husband as he dropped two lumps of sugar into the cup of tea in front of him. "He did, didn't he? And you said you'd cover for him."

Archie ran his hands through his thick mane of greying hair. "I'm sorry, but his need sounded greater than mine. Let's be honest, I was never going to fit in this weekend, was

I? Your father already looks down on me and with all those lords and ladies around..."

"Is that what this is about? After all these years, can't you bear to spend time with my father?"

"Of course I can, but ... well, he doesn't make it easy, does he? You'll be spending all weekend with his best friend, whose daughter happened to marry an earl. He'll have more reason than usual to sneer at me. I'm better off staying here."

"That's nonsense, it's all in your imagination. Father wouldn't do that. He never once criticised Henry when he decided to study medicine." Eliza perched on the edge of a chair. "And talking of Henry, you do realise he'll be there this weekend and we haven't seen him for months."

Archie put a hand to his head. "I'd completely forgotten. Why don't you ask him to come here for a week? He can't be due back at university for another week or two."

Eliza groaned. "You know what he'll think of that idea. It's as if he wants nothing to do with us since we moved out of London. I was hoping you'd be able to talk to him."

Archie reached for her hand. "He'll be back when he wants more money, you mark my words. I'll tell you what, why don't you still go? I don't want to spoil it for you."

"On my own?"

"Your father will be on his own, won't he?"

Eliza shook her head. "That's different and you know it. Besides, I can't travel on the train by myself."

Archie shook his head. "No, you're right. I'll tell you what, why don't you invite Connie? I'm sure Caroline won't mind."

"Connie?"

2

"Why not? You do almost everything else together. I'm sure she'd enjoy seeing how the ruling class live."

"But the family dinner's tomorrow night. It's rather short notice."

A frown settled on Archie's forehead. "Don't you want her to go?"

"Yes, of course, it's not that, but ... well, she likes to plan things and she's been complaining that her dresses are looking dated. I'm not sure she'll want to spend the weekend in a stately home, especially not with there being a ball on Saturday evening."

Archie stood up and took a final mouthful from his cup of tea. "You're about the same size, aren't you? Why don't you lend her one of your ballgowns?"

Eliza sighed. "I suppose I could, if she wouldn't mind, but what will Caroline think? She'll have been working on the seating arrangements for weeks and if I arrive with Connie instead of you..."

"Connie can just take my seat. I imagine that would be preferable to cancelling the whole weekend."

Eliza nodded slowly. "I'll need to send Caroline a telegram and tell her what's happening. I hope she doesn't mind."

Archie smiled. "That's settled then. I'll tell you what, I don't have many appointments this morning, why don't you go and speak to Connie and I'll deal with the patients?"

Eliza grinned. He always knew he could get around her with that soft Scottish accent. "As long as you can remember how to make up the creams and lotions."

Archie narrowed his eyes at her. "I'll have less of your

cheek. Now be off with you. Go and tell Connie the good news."

Connie stood in the middle of her living room, her eyes wide as she gazed at Eliza.

"Me? Spend a weekend in a stately home... and go to a debutante ball?"

"Why not?"

"Why not? Because I'm Mrs Connie Appleton, a widow and lifelong resident of Moreton-on-Thames, that's why not. I won't know anyone, let alone know what to say to them."

"It's not what you think. Father will be there, and you remember him, and Lady Caroline was just plain Miss Caroline Brough before she married the earl. Even before we were born, my father and hers were the best of friends. Father is her godfather. There's nothing fancy about them."

"So how did she end up marrying an earl?"

Eliza rolled her eyes and took a seat by the fireside. "We used to go to school together, but when I left to go to university, she went to a finishing school in Switzerland."

"What on earth did her father do to make his money?"

"He produced steel for the railways; that's how he knew Father. The problem was, as he made more money, her mother became determined that Caroline should marry well. When she came home from Switzerland, Mrs Brough, as she was then, made it her business to get Caroline on the invitation list for as many debutante balls as she could. Although she wasn't presented to the Queen, she met Lord Lowton at one of the balls and married him six months later."

Connie smiled as her head fell to one side. "Lucky her.

And so the debutante ball is for their daughter? Has she been presented to the King yet?"

"I don't think so. The season only started a couple of weeks ago but with the Queen dying, the Palace had to delay the presentations."

"I hadn't thought of that."

"Not that it's stopped the season. It's still back-to-back parties from now until August."

Connie puffed out her cheeks. "It must be a glamorous life."

"Yes, very. Not to mention expensive. I'm glad I'm only going to one ball." Eliza stood up and walked to the window. "If you're coming with me, I need to go to the post office and send Caroline a telegram to tell her what's happening. What do you say?"

"I don't know..."

"Oh, please. It'll be fun."

Connie fidgeted with the bow on the front of her dress. "Are you sure Lady Caroline won't mind?"

Eliza smiled. "I'm sure she won't."

"And you don't mind lending me a couple of dresses?"

"Not at all."

"All right then, I suppose so."

Eliza clapped her hands together. "Excellent. Now, come along and get your coat on before those rain clouds move in ... and you change your mind."

CHAPTER TWO

It was three o'clock when the train pulled into Lowton railway station, three quarters of an hour after it had left Moreton-on-Thames, and Eliza noticed Connie tighten her grip on the handbag perched on her knee.

"Don't look so frightened."

Connie's usually pale complexion was decidedly white. "It's all right for you, you know these people."

"Only Caroline and her mother and father, I don't know the rest of the family ... well, not very well anyway."

"But you've met them?"

"Not all of them. I saw Lord Lowton several times when I visited Caroline at their Mayfair house, not that he had time to talk to the likes of me. I met him at the marriage service as well, although thinking about it, that was an 'us and them' situation. They've been married for over twenty years now though and so I'm sure that will be behind them. Underneath everything, they're only people like us, who happen to have more money."

"And bigger houses."

Eliza nodded. "And bigger houses."

"And power."

Eliza squeezed Connie's hand. "Stop worrying, this is our stop. Hopefully, someone will be here to take us to Lowton Hall and then you'll see."

Ten minutes later, a horse-drawn carriage bearing the coat of arms of the earl of Lowton turned into the driveway of Lowton Hall. Connie couldn't keep her eyes from the window.

"Look at the trees, you can't even see the house yet."

Eliza sighed. "You'd have seen it quicker if they'd sent their new motor car to pick us up. I know I shouldn't be ungrateful, but I had hoped they would. Wouldn't that be fun... to go in such a splendid machine? It would have served Archie right as well for cancelling on me."

Connie gasped. "Oh, my word. Have you seen the hall?"

Eliza put her face to the window and gazed out at the stone-and-glass facade as it emerged from the trees. The central four-storey section stood proudly at the head of the stone driveway, flanked on either side by well-tended lawns. It bore an ornate bell tower high above the front door and to either side rooms led to the two wings of the house.

"At least there shouldn't be a problem finding you a spare bedroom," Eliza said.

Connie clenched her handbag again. "I hope I've not put them to any trouble. You will explain, won't you?"

With the carriage at a standstill, the coachman appeared from the back and opened the door before arranging the steps for them to climb down. At the same moment, the front door opened and a man Eliza presumed to be the butler stepped out to greet them.

"Mrs Thomson and Mrs Appleton, I presume. Please follow me. Lady Caroline is expecting you."

The butler waited by the door, his left arm extended towards the hallway.

"What about the bags?" Connie turned around in search of her luggage.

"Leave it," Eliza whispered. "They'll send them straight to the rooms. You won't have to do anything while you're here."

They followed the butler across a large square hallway where an elaborate central staircase gave them both reason to pause.

"Look at that." Connie's voice was breathless as she gazed up at a splendid crystal chandelier. "It would fill my living room."

Eliza grinned at her friend as the butler continued to a highly polished pair of mahogany doors set to the right-hand side of the stairs. He gave a brisk knock before pushing them open and ushering the ladies inside.

"Your guests, m'lady."

Eliza smiled as she spotted a small group seated around the fireplace.

"Eliza!" A petite woman with deep brown eyes and an elaborate chignon of dark hair hurried towards them and took Eliza's hands. "How lovely to see you again, it's been too long, and your friend Mrs Appleton, I presume."

"It is. Lady Caroline, this is Connie; Connie, this is Lady Caroline. Archie sends his apologies for cancelling so late in the day."

"I'm sure we'll miss him, but think nothing of it." Lady Caroline held out a hand to Connie, who gave a curtsey.

"Thank you for having me. What a lovely room."

Eliza nodded in agreement as she admired the wall of floor-to-ceiling windows that overlooked the gardens, allowing sunlight to flood in.

"Yes, isn't it?" Caroline ran her eyes around the room. "Although it's far too big for everyday use. We only come in here when we have guests, but between you and me, it gets awfully draughty. That's why we're sitting by the fire. Come and join us. I think you know everyone, Eliza."

They approached the fireplace as a tall, slim man with grey-blond hair and matching moustache stood up to greet them.

"Father." Eliza smiled as he wrapped his arms around her. "I wasn't expecting you to be here yet."

"I've got more time on my hands since I retired, so I took the two o'clock train. Besides, I don't see nearly enough of you now you've moved back to Moreton and so I wanted to be early."

"Well, I'm glad you are. You remember Connie, don't you?"

"Of course I do." Mr Bell took Connie's hand and kissed it. "How delightful to see you again. I didn't realise you were joining us."

Connie flashed him a smile. "I'm here in place of Dr Thomson."

Mr Bell studied his daughter. "Why isn't he here? Has he let you travel up here on your own?"

"He took us to the station and helped us onto the train. He couldn't join us because the doctor in the neighbouring village needed to go away at short notice and someone has to cover."

"And it had to be him. When's he going to get a respectable job?"

Eliza took a deep breath. "You know that being a doctor is becoming more acceptable. You'll be glad of one when you're ill."

"If you say so." Mr Bell shook his head before turning towards the couple sitting behind him. "Now, you remember Lady Caroline's parents, don't you?"

Eliza smiled. "Of course, Mr and Mrs Brough. It's been a long time."

Mr Bell's eyes widened. "Not Mr and Mrs, Sir Rodney and Lady Brough, if you don't mind."

"Lady Rosemary is quite acceptable." Lady Brough smiled as Eliza put a hand to her mouth.

"Yes, I'm sorry, how remiss of me. Congratulations. It's quite an honour."

"Nothing more than Rodney deserved," Mr Bell said.

"I didn't deserve it any more than you." Sir Rodney stood up and first kissed Eliza's hand followed by Connie's. "I must speak to Neville about your knighthood, George, see what he can do for you."

"That would be jolly decent of you, old chap," Mr Bell said.

"Neville is Lord Lowton to us," Eliza whispered to Connie as she guided her to a chair next to Sir Rodney before taking the seat by her father.

"Is Lord Lowton not joining us?" Eliza asked.

"Oh, he'll be here soon enough." Lady Caroline placed

two cups of tea on a table near them. "He had some work he wanted to go through with his solicitor and so they're in his office. Now, come and sit down and help yourself to some cake. We've got more important things to catch up on than Neville."

With all the tea, and most of the cakes gone, the ornate clock on the mantelpiece struck five o'clock.

"My goodness, is that the time?" Lady Caroline stood up. "Please stay in here as long as you wish, but I need to go. With twelve coming for dinner I need to check the dining room and sort myself out before everyone arrives. We're meeting in here at half past seven for a sherry with dinner at eight."

Eliza watched her walk to the door, but before she reached the handle, it opened from the other side and two young men entered.

"Here you are, Albert." Lady Caroline spoke to the shorter of the two with a mop of mousy brown hair. "I was beginning to wonder what had happened to you. Is Alice with you?"

"She's gone to her room. Said she needed to lie down."

"Oh, the poor thing. She must be exhausted with everything that's happening this weekend. I must go and see her."

"Henry!" Eliza joined Lady Caroline by the door and planted a kiss on the cheek of a young man who was the image of Archie. "We were just talking about you. Did you have a good time in London?"

A grin spread across Henry's lips as he grinned at Lord Albert. "Very nice, thank you. Is there any tea left?"

"Let me get you some." Eliza stepped towards the door before stopping. "May I do that, Caroline?"

Lady Caroline laughed. "I daresay you could, but let me, I'm off to find Soams anyway. He's our butler." She turned to Albert. "You and Henry take a seat and I'll get some sent in."

"Well, this is nice," Eliza said as she followed them back to their seats and made the relevant introductions.

"Is Father not here?" Henry asked Eliza. "I was hoping to speak to him."

"No, he couldn't leave the village without a doctor. Can I help?"

Henry's shoulders slumped. "No, it doesn't matter. It looks like I'll have to travel back to Moreton with you."

"How lovely."

"Tell me about Cambridge then." Mr Bell spoke to both boys. "Are you studying medicine as well, Lord Albert?"

"No, agriculture. I'll be in charge of the estate one day, so I need to be prepared."

"Albert's more than capable, aren't you, my boy?" Sir Rodney smiled fondly at his grandson.

"Naturally, Father's been teaching me since I was a child. Now, where's that tea?" Lord Albert strode to the door and down the hall.

"He seems a very ... confident boy," Eliza said.

"He has to be, given the life he has ahead of him," Henry said. "All he has to do is snap his fingers and he gets whatever he wants."

"You can't blame him for that," Lady Rosemary said. "He *is* being trained to be an earl."

"You don't do so badly, Henry Thomson, and don't you forget it." Eliza studied her son before standing up. "Right, it's about time Connie and I dressed for dinner. We'll see you later."

Eliza and Connie left the room and followed a footman upstairs.

"Are you all right?" Connie asked as they reached the upper landing.

"I'll be fine, it's just Henry. He's become so distant since he went to Cambridge, and judging by that little performance, I'd say Lord Albert's arrogance is wearing off on him."

"He was fine, he's probably just showing off. If he's anything like me, he must feel overwhelmed next to Lord Albert."

"Perhaps, although that's not like him either."

"Here you are, ladies." The footman stopped outside a bedroom door before holding it open. "Lady Caroline's given you rooms with a connecting sitting room."

"How thoughtful." Connie clasped her hands to her chest as they followed the footman into a florally decorated area replete with a settee and two armchairs.

"Mrs Thomson, your bedroom is through the door to your right." He walked to the far corner and held a door open for Eliza. "Mrs Appleton, you're in the room to the left. You can ring the bell in the sitting room if you need anything."

With a slight bow, the footman left them and as the door closed, they both did a full turn in the sitting room before inspecting both bedrooms.

"My goodness, it's bigger than my whole house," Connie said.

"And what a wonderful view too. Is that a lake out there beyond the formal lawns?"

"I'd say so. I do hope we get a chance to have a wander around while we're here."

CHAPTER THREE

Soams waited in the entrance hall as Eliza and Connie made their way down the sweeping staircase on their way to dinner. He hovered around the bottom step and gave a slight bow as they joined him.

"Good evening, ladies. His Lordship and Lady Caroline are waiting for you in the drawing room." He extended an arm towards an open door as he led the way. "Mrs Thomson and Mrs Appleton," he announced before stepping backwards out of the room.

"Eliza, Mrs Appleton, here you are," Lady Caroline said. "Let me introduce you to Neville."

Lady Caroline headed towards a stout man with auburn hair and a magnificent handlebar moustache.

"Neville, this is Eliza, you remember me telling you about her, and her companion Mrs Appleton."

Following Connie's lead, Eliza gave her best curtsey as Lord Lowton offered her his hand.

"How nice to meet you. My wife's told me a lot about you."

Eliza could feel her cheeks flushing. "It's a pleasure to meet you again, Your Lordship. It's been several years since we met in Mayfair."

The blank look on Lord Lowton's face suggested he didn't remember the encounter, but he quickly regained his composure. "Yes, of course. Naturally, we'll be moving back there next week for the rest of the season, once we've got Alice's ball out of the way."

Eliza smiled at Lady Caroline as Lord Lowton turned away. "Are we the last here?"

With a quick scan of the room, Lady Caroline nodded. "You are, but only by a minute. In case you're wondering where Henry is, I said the children could dine on their own tonight. I'm sure they'll enjoy it more. Now, let me get you a drink before I introduce you to everyone."

As if by some hidden signal, a maid stepped forward carrying a tray of sherry glasses and Lady Caroline handed Eliza and Connie a glass each before taking one for herself.

"Now, where to start? I suppose it had better be with my brother-in-law." Lady Caroline walked towards a huddle of men all in evening dress. "Excuse me, gentlemen, may I introduce my friends, Mrs Thomson and Mrs Appleton? Mrs Thomson is Mr Bell's daughter and is here for the weekend with her companion. Eliza, this is the Honourable Cyril Lowton, Neville's brother."

A man with the same receding hairline as Lord Lowton, but with a more manageable moustache, stepped forward and bowed towards them.

"Good evening, ladies, it's very nice to meet you. May I introduce my brother-in-law, Lord Forsyth, and our family lawyer, Lord Beaufort?"

Eliza and Connie once again curtsied.

"There's no need to be so formal, my dears," Lady Caroline said. "We're all family here ... well, actually Lord Beaufort isn't, but he's here to see Neville most days and we've known him so long he might as well be."

A rotund man with a shiny red face shook his head. "I've not been here so much recently, not since I got my appointment."

"No, you've not." Lady Caroline patted Lord Beaufort on the shoulder. "He became a law lord earlier in the year and now spends most of the week in London. Neville doesn't know what to do with himself when he's not here."

Lord Beaufort chuckled. "He's been talking about taking up his seat in the House of Lords more frequently to keep in touch."

"That doesn't surprise me," Lady Caroline said, "although I've no idea who'll manage the estate if he's not here. Perhaps you could do it, Cyril?"

Lady Caroline smiled and raised an eyebrow at her brother-in-law, but his face stiffened.

"I have my own arrangements to attend to, thank you; I don't need to do anyone else's work." He emptied his sherry glass and pushed past Lady Caroline as he headed towards the maid.

Lady Caroline smirked at Lord Beaufort before she steered her guests back to the middle of the room. "Don't mind him. He gets a tad touchy about the fact Neville inherited the estate and title and he got nothing. You'd think he'd be used to it by now."

"Does he still live here?" Connie asked.

"Good grief, no. Not that he wouldn't like to, but when I

arrived here as a new bride, Neville told him he had to move into his own house. He lives in a cottage on the estate now, but he's never forgiven me for pushing him out." Lady Caroline grinned and Eliza smirked when she saw the glint in her eye.

"He probably didn't like the fact you were a commoner either."

Lady Caroline threw her head back as she laughed. "Don't even mention that, he was furious. He kept saying that his father would never have allowed the marriage, but as the old man was dead and Neville was the new earl, he could do as he pleased."

"What are you looking so cheerful about?" An exquisitely dressed lady who Eliza guessed was in her late forties stepped forward and smiled at Lady Caroline.

"I'm just telling my friends here about your little brother."

The stranger grinned at Lady Caroline before extending her hand to Eliza. "Lady Hilda Forsyth, delighted to meet you."

Eliza was mid-curtsey before she remembered she needn't bother. She straightened up quickly and accepted the hand being offered to her. "Your Ladyship, I'm Eliza Thomson, an old friend of Caroline's, and this is my friend Mrs Connie Appleton. Pleased to meet you too."

"Hilda will present Alice to His Majesty in June." Lady Caroline beamed at her sister-in-law.

"Won't you do it yourself?" Connie asked.

"Oh, my dear, I wish I could, but rules are rules. You can only present someone to His Majesty if someone presented you. Mother was good enough to get me into the balls, but I never made it to the Palace myself."

"It helped having an earl as a father," Lady Hilda said. "In my day, most of us were selected for presentation. It's much harder nowadays. I shouldn't like to be the daughter of a mere baron."

"Or of an honourable gentleman." Lady Caroline couldn't hide the glee in her eyes as she glanced over at Sir Cyril.

"Does he have a daughter?" Eliza asked, following Lady Caroline's gaze.

"He does, Lady Mary. A nice girl considering..."

Eliza's forehead creased but before she could open her mouth, Lady Caroline answered the question on her lips.

"The title's from her mother's side of the family. Just to rub salt into the wound, Cyril's wife, Lady Victoria, is the eldest daughter of an earl."

Eliza nodded. "I can see these little details keep you amused."

"Oh, we need something, don't we, Hilda? Besides, Cyril asks for it."

Hilda laughed. "Have they met Victoria yet?"

"Not yet, but she looks bored talking to Lady Beaufort. Shall we go over?"

They walked towards the fireplace and a settee that held the curvaceous figure of a woman who, in her youth, must have been beautiful.

"Victoria," Lady Caroline said. "May I introduce you to my friends?"

Lady Victoria fixed a smile on her face but didn't stand up. "Welcome. Are you here for the weekend?"

Eliza shuddered and held her arms in front of her as Lady Victoria's deep blue eyes ran over her evening dress. "We are. My father, Mr Bell, is Lady Caroline's godfather."

"Ah, it makes sense now. Well, I'm sure I'll see you around." She pushed herself up from the settee. "I must get another sherry before dinner."

"I don't know why she needs another one," Lady Caroline whispered once she was out of earshot. "She knows she won't be sitting next to Cyril at dinner. They must have had another row."

"Oh dear, who has that pleasure then?" Connie asked.

Lady Caroline's face paled. "I'm sorry to say but you do, my dear. I originally put dear Archie next to him and I haven't been able to change the seating. Don't worry, I'll be on your other side."

Connie nodded. "Where will Eliza be sitting?"

"Didn't I tell you?" Eliza noticed the twinkle in Lady Caroline's eyes. "Because of the way these things work, you're our female guest of honour and so you're on Neville's right-hand side."

"I'm a guest of honour? Really?" Eliza scrutinised those in the room. "But Connie and I must be the only untitled ladies."

"Ah, that doesn't matter. You're one of the few who aren't family and that's what counts."

Eliza nodded as a shiver ran down her spine. "Who's on my other side?"

"Don't worry, I thought you might need some light relief and so I've put my father next to you. Just help yourself to another sherry and have a couple of glasses of wine with dinner and you'll be fine."

The chimes of the synchronised clocks rang out for eight o'clock as the gong sounded to announce that dinner was imminent. Under Lady Caroline's direction, the guests lined up to parade to the dining room and Eliza found herself at the head of the line with Lord Lowton on her left. *Why on earth was I so excited about coming? This is positively nerve-wracking.*

Lord Lowton checked over his shoulder, and once the guests were all in position, he took Eliza's arm. "Are you ready? The dining room is out into the hall and then we turn left towards the west wing. No need to be nervous."

Eliza struggled to keep her grip on His Lordship's arm light as they walked through the corridors, but within a minute she saw the double doors to the dining room were already open. Lord Lowton escorted her to the far end of the room and stood at the head of the oval table with Eliza to his right.

As the rest of the party filed in after them, Eliza examined her name card before turning her attention to the rest of the table. It was set with an array of knives, forks and glasses, and Eliza peered across at Connie hoping she would be familiar with such formal dining.

"There's an odd number of guests, Caroline ... and thirteen at that." Sir Cyril projected his voice across the room as he approached the table. "Have you learned nothing in twenty years of marriage?"

Lady Caroline glared at her brother-in-law. "If it's not too much trouble, perhaps you could start the seating?"

With a loud harrumph, Sir Cyril turned to his left-hand side and held out the chair for Lady Rosemary. Once she was seated, he turned to his right to repeat the movement for

Connie. With Connie seated, Eliza gave a sigh of relief, before realising that Lord Lowton was hovering behind her waiting for her to take her own seat.

"Thank you." She looked down the table to signal to Connie, but the smile fell from her face when she realised that the arrangements of flowers and candelabras lining the centre of the table were partially shielding her view.

She considered adjusting her chair but a footman appeared by her side holding a bottle of white wine. "Wine, madam?"

"Oh yes, please. Only a little though."

"Do you drink wine often?" His Lordship asked as the footman moved around the table.

"No, not at all," Eliza said. "I usually stick to sherry."

"Well, I hope you enjoy it. It's a particularly fine vintage."

Eliza nodded but left the glass where it was. "I'm sure it will be lovely."

"So your husband couldn't join you?" Lord Lowton said. "Most unfortunate."

"Yes, it was. He's a doctor, you see, and couldn't get away."

"I suppose somebody has to do the work," Lord Lowton blustered. "Still, I'd have expected him to accompany you."

Eliza picked up her glass and took a mouthful of wine. "Yes, he sends his apologies."

"This is a very important weekend, you know."

"Yes, I'm sure." Eliza glanced around the table. "Am I right in thinking you have a sister who isn't here?"

"Damn stupid woman. She should be here. It's that husband of hers ... the Marquess of Hastings. He decided

22

two years ago to spend the winter in Egypt of all places, and apparently this year the warm weather's been so appealing they've extended their stay until the end of the month. Why they've chosen to stay there rather than join us, I'll never know. They didn't even have the decency to tell Caroline in good time. We only got the letter on Wednesday when it was too late to invite anyone else."

"What a shame, especially missing Lady Alice's ball."

"Quite. You would think their niece's coming-out ball would be worth coming home for, but the marquess has strange ideas of family life. He never puts anyone before himself and I'm sure my sister's protestations would have been minimal."

With a final harrumph, Lord Lowton turned to Lady Beaufort on his left giving Eliza time to glance around the rest of the table.

"Is this the first time you've dined here?" Sir Rodney asked from her other side.

"Yes, it is, although I suppose you're used to all this pomp and ceremony nowadays."

Sir Rodney chuckled. "Not really, to tell you the truth. We still live in our modest house in London. We're only here a couple of times a year. Just often enough to know why anyone requires five sets of knives and forks for a simple dinner."

Eliza giggled before glancing across the table towards Connie. *I should have warned her*. At least from what she could see she seemed happy enough to be talking to Lady Caroline. It was probably a blessing that Sir Cyril had chosen to sit with his back to her as he spoke with Lady Rosemary.

Sir Rodney nodded towards his wife. "Don't worry, she

can take care of herself. We've had enough run-ins with Cyril over the years to know not to take him seriously."

Eliza grimaced. "I'm sure you have, but it's my friend I'm worried about. I hope Caroline looks after her."

It was almost ten o'clock before the dessert dishes were tidied away and Lady Caroline invited the ladies to join her in the drawing room for coffee. Despite a pleasant enough evening, Eliza was painfully aware of Sir Cyril's frequent outbursts and she was keen to hear what Connie had to say about him.

"Thank you for a lovely evening," she said to Lord Lowton as he helped her from her chair.

"You're most welcome. I'm sure we'll see each other again tomorrow."

Soams was waiting to help with her chair and as she left, she heard Lord Lowton ask him to request the company of the young men over coffee. *Henry. Of course. I wonder what he's been up to this evening.*

By the time Eliza left the room, Connie was ahead of her talking to Lady Rosemary and she hurried to catch them up. She hadn't reached the main entrance hall when she heard Sir Cyril's voice bellowing from the staircase. She rounded the corner to see the honourable gentleman towering over Henry as he cowered on a settee that ran along the back wall. Taking a deep breath, she stepped forward.

"What on earth's going on here?"

Sir Cyril swung around to face her. "Is this your son?" He didn't wait for a reply before he continued. "In case you weren't aware, Lady Alice will be presented to His Majesty in a matter of weeks. My brother has gone to considerable expense to host a ball for her tomorrow evening and in the coming months we hope to find a suitable husband for her. Cavorting with the likes of ... *him* is not the behaviour I expect to encounter."

Eliza glowered at her son.

"We weren't doing anything." Henry's deep brown eyes were wide.

"You were sitting on the stairs together looking far too intimate." Sir Cyril's face was puce. "Now, get out of here."

Eliza's heart skipped a beat at the sight of several veins throbbing in Sir Cyril's neck.

"Y-yes, you need to go. I believe Lord Lowton would like you and Lord Albert ... and your other friend, to join him in the dining room."

Henry needed no further prompting and along with his friends hurried across the hall towards the west wing.

"That other friend is my son Lord David, and at least he has the decency to know how to behave. The future of this family depends on my nephew and niece marrying into the best aristocratic families we can find. My brother has already lessened their blood by marrying a commoner and I will not have his progeny demeaning our family name further."

Eliza and Connie stood with their mouths open as Sir Cyril charged up the stairs.

"What on earth happened?" Eliza said once he was out of sight.

Lady Caroline emerged from behind them, her face scarlet and nostrils flared. "He's gone too far this time. Who on earth does he think he is? This is my weekend as much as Alice's and I will not let him ruin it. If Neville won't get rid of him in the morning, then as God is my witness, I will."

CHAPTER FOUR

E liza flinched at the sound of the knock on her bedroom door and turned away from the window.

"Come in." She rubbed her hands across her face as Connie's head appeared around the door.

"Oh good, you're dressed ... but you look awful. How are you feeling?"

"I've been better, I didn't sleep a wink last night." She shook her head. "What was Henry thinking?"

"He probably wasn't thinking anything. Besides, as I told you last night, when I saw them on the stairs all they were doing was laughing together."

"I can't help worrying that you didn't see everything. I've never seen Caroline so angry either. I hope it was all directed at Sir Cyril and not at me or Henry."

"Of course it was, she said so herself. Now, shall we go down to breakfast? Hopefully, everyone will have calmed down."

Eliza nodded. "I suppose so, we have to face them sooner or later."

As they walked into the breakfast room, a cold chill ran down Eliza's spine. Sitting at the head of the table, talking to Lord Beaufort was Sir Cyril. She stopped in the doorway but breathed a sigh of relief as her father beckoned her over.

"Eliza, Connie, come and join me." He stood up and held out a chair for each of them. "I didn't get a chance to speak to you last night." He retook the seat next to Eliza.

"No, I suppose that's the problem with these formal gatherings."

With a withering look at Eliza, Sir Cyril stood up. "What would you know about formal gatherings?"

"I beg your pardon," Mr Bell said. "You may have a title, but it doesn't entitle you to talk to a lady like that. Apologise at once."

"It's she who should apologise to me after the behaviour of her son last night. Hasn't she told you about him?"

Mr Bell turned to Eliza, his eyes wide. "What happened?"

"There's nothing to tell." Eliza returned Sir Cyril's glare. "Do you always cause such a drama when people are enjoying themselves?"

"What's going on here?" Lady Caroline's face was like thunder as she walked into the room.

"Don't you start, this is all your doing." Sir Cyril threw his napkin onto the table and stomped to the door. "Father should have forbidden Neville from marrying the likes of you, even if he'd had to write it in his Last Will and Testament."

"How dare you? Get out of here now and don't bother coming back," Lady Caroline called after him, but he slammed the door behind him.

Mr Bell jumped to his feet ready to go after him, but Eliza held out an arm. "Please don't, come and finish your breakfast. It's clear he doesn't like our sort and nothing you say will make him change his mind."

Mr Bell stared at the door before retaking his seat. "If he thinks he can speak to you or Caroline like that and get away with it, he can think again. Wait until the next time I see him."

"Please, enough of him," Lady Caroline said. "I've spoken to Neville and hopefully that will be the last we see of him. I've got far more important things on my mind than worrying about the tantrums of the youngest son of an earl."

"How are the preparations going for tonight?" Connie asked as the silence in the room deepened.

Lady Caroline closed her eyes and took a breath. "They'll be fine once the florists have the good grace to turn up and Cook lets the additional help into the kitchen. Honestly, I told her yesterday they'd be here by eight o'clock, but she refuses to let them into the kitchen until she's cleared away the breakfast dishes."

"I'm sure everything will be fine. At least the kitchen workers are here, and the florists can't be far away. They won't want to miss an event like this."

"Connie's right," Eliza said. "Let me get you a cup of tea and we'll finish here and get out of the way. It looks like a lovely day for a walk in the grounds ... if you don't mind."

Lady Caroline gave a feeble smile. "Of course I don't mind, I want you to enjoy yourself. I'm sorry, it's just that this is the biggest event I've ever put on, and there will be many others like Cyril who want me to fail."

"I'm sure that's not true."

Lord Beaufort, who had finished his breakfast in silence, pushed himself up from the table. "Sadly, I know only too well that Caroline is right. There are plenty who are furious that the likes of us are breaking into their inner circle, but don't worry, Neville will deal with them. I'll see you later."

Breakfast couldn't finish quickly enough for Eliza, and as soon as they could get away, she and Connie hurried upstairs to put on their hats and coats. Within five minutes they returned to join Mr Bell in the conservatory. At such an early hour, the sun remained hidden behind the east wing and Eliza shivered as she went in.

"Are you ready?" she asked her father.

"I am." He pushed himself up from an armchair and wandered over to a glazed door that overlooked the garden. "We can get out here."

The air was bright and crisp as they stepped onto the terrace.

"What a fabulous view," Connie said as they stopped to take in the expanse of formal gardens. "We could spend the next hour just walking around this section of the estate."

Eliza took a deep breath and smiled. "Why don't we start with the path down the left side of the lawn? It looks like it will take us to the lake, and you said you'd like to walk around it."

Connie's face lit up. "Lead the way then."

"I wonder how many gardeners they need to keep all this tidy," Mr Bell said as they walked down the steps to the footpath.

"I can't begin to imagine, it must be dozens," Eliza said.

"Well, I'm glad it's their garden and not mine. That's one of the attractions of living in Richmond, I get a house in London and a park less than five minutes away ... tended by someone else."

Connie laughed. "So you won't be moving back to Moreton then, Mr Bell?"

"Not at the moment, although I will come and visit. I haven't been since Eliza moved back. What's all this about Henry, anyway? I obviously missed something last night."

Eliza groaned and explained what had happened.

"And did Henry give an account of what he'd been doing?"

Eliza shook her head. "No, Lord Lowton had requested the company of the younger men, and so I sent him there immediately to get him out of the way. I've not seen him this morning."

"It's about time Archie had a word with him," Mr Bell said. "He needs a firm hand. He's changed since I last saw him."

"You've noticed it too?" Eliza said. "I thought it was just me. If you want my opinion, it's since he started at Cambridge ... although perhaps Lord Albert's had some influence on him."

"Do you think he was up to no good with Lady Alice?" Mr Bell asked.

Eliza shrugged. "Who knows, Connie says not, but by the time we arrived in the hallway Sir Cyril was already there. I suppose it's possible he may have disturbed something. Didn't Sir Cyril mention anything about it when he returned to the dining room last night?"

Mr Bell shook his head. "No, not a word, although

thinking about it, Henry took your seat beside Lord Lowton, and so maybe Sir Cyril knew better than to say anything."

"Well, whatever happened I hope Henry's learned his lesson."

"And that Lord Lowton can get rid of Sir Cyril before the ball tonight." Connie shuddered. "I'd rather not spend another evening in his company."

"If Caroline has anything to do with it, I don't think you need worry on that score," Eliza said. "Why don't we just forget about him and enjoy the walk?"

They continued in agreeable silence until they neared the end of the formal garden where the landscape transformed into a small woodland area that surrounded the lake.

"Look at the flowers on those magnificent bushes," Connie said. "Rhododendrons, aren't they? I love that deep shade of pink."

"And look at the size of the lake," Eliza said. "It's bigger than I imagined. It will take us at least an hour to walk around it."

Connie gazed out over the water. "I'm sure we have time. Lady Caroline said luncheon isn't being served until half past twelve. It can't be any later than half past ten now."

Mr Bell checked his pocket watch. "Twenty-eight minutes past to be precise."

"There you go, that should be plenty of time," Connie said. "Shall we go?"

"Wait a moment." Mr Bell hastily pushed his watch back into his pocket. "Is that Sir Cyril by the rhododendrons? I want a word with him. You start walking around the lake and I'll catch you up."

"No, Father, please don't..." Eliza called after Mr Bell, but he had already set off down a path towards the bushes. "It's not worth it."

"I don't think he heard," Connie said. "Should we follow him?"

Eliza glanced at the lake and then back at her father, who was approaching the spot he'd seen Sir Cyril. "Yes, come on. I don't want him getting into any trouble."

Eliza and Connie strolled along the path Mr Bell had taken, stopping to admire the view as they rounded the bend near the rhododendron bushes.

"It's like being in another world, isn't it?" Connie said. "Despite the antics with Sir Cyril, I'm so glad you persuaded me to come with you. Reading magazine articles about houses like this doesn't do them justice."

"No, you're right."

They continued walking but stopped abruptly when a shout rang out from behind the bushes.

"Over here, someone come quickly."

"That's Father!" Without thinking Eliza hitched up the front of her skirt and hurried to the other side of the bushes. "Father, what is it...?" She rounded the corner but stopped in her tracks as she saw Mr Bell standing in the lake, waist deep in water. Lords Lowton and Albert knelt on the bank on either side of him. A second later, Connie crashed into the back of her.

"What is it? Oh my, who's that?" Connie's eyes were fixed on Mr Bell as he pushed a body up out of the water.

"Get a move on, man." Lord Lowton grappled with the torso as he struggled to pull it onto the bank. "Albert, get a proper grip."

With Lord Albert's help, the body moved forward onto the bank causing Mr Bell to topple backwards. He was on the verge of losing his balance when he grabbed for the reeds at the edge of the lake. Eliza lurched forward to offer him her hand, but as he reached out to catch hold of her, his fingers brushed a croquet mallet hidden in the reeds. It was wedged firm and at the second attempt, he caught it and pulled himself to the water's edge.

With a sigh of relief, Eliza grasped her father's hand and helped him from the water before turning her attention to the body Lord Lowton had managed to pull from the water. "Oh, my goodness." The bile rose from her stomach. "It's Sir Cyril. Is he dead?"

CHAPTER FIVE

Lord Lowton and his son pulled the body away from the water onto the footpath, and by the time Mr Bell joined them, Lord Lowton had turned it over onto its back.

"We need a doctor," Eliza said.

"No, no doctor. Not today." Lord Lowton put one knee to the ground alongside his brother's head and ran his fingers over the lifeless eyelids. "No doctor can save him now; it can wait."

"I'm so sorry," Connie said. "Do we know what happened?"

Lord Lowton stared at his brother, but said nothing.

"He was already in the water when I found him," Mr Bell said. "As I approached the bushes, I heard a noise followed by a splash and rushed around to find him. Their Lordships followed close behind me."

"That's right," Lord Albert said.

"You'll need a doctor to certify the death. We can't leave him here," Eliza said.

Lord Lowton snapped to his senses. "You're right, we

can't. Albert, go and find one of the gardeners and ask them to bring something to move the body in. They can put it in the folly at the far end of the lake for now. It's the only one that has a door that locks." Lord Lowton put a hand in his pocket and pulled out a bunch of keys. "Here, take these and be quick about it."

"You can't do that…" Eliza said, but Lord Albert disappeared, paying her no attention.

"My dear, today is the day of my daughter's coming-out ball. You've already seen how highly strung Caroline is about it. Something like this would be too much for her."

"But you can't leave a dead body lying in a folly overnight."

Lord Lowton glared at her. "Do you have any idea how infrequently people walk around this part of the garden? If your father hadn't passed this way, my brother could easily have lain in the water overnight. Putting him in the folly is preferable to that, wouldn't you say? Now, I'll have no more arguing. We'll tell the guests at the house that Cyril was feeling ill and that he's taken himself home to bed."

"But what about Lady Victoria … and their son and daughter? You'll need to tell them the truth. You can't pretend this hasn't happened."

Lord Lowton flinched at the mention of his sister-in-law. "I'll tell Lady Victoria myself, but other than her, nobody else must know. Not today. I don't want a word of this uttered in the house until I announce it tomorrow morning. Have I made myself clear?"

Under His Lordship's glare, Eliza had no choice but to nod, and within a minute he was striding away from the lake in the direction of the path to the right-hand side of the lawn.

Once he disappeared behind the bushes Eliza stared down at Sir Cyril.

"The poor man. We might have had our differences, but I wouldn't wish this on anyone. I wonder what happened."

"I've told you all I know," Mr Bell said.

"What's this?" Eliza crouched down beside the body and put her fingers in some dark liquid beneath Sir Cyril's head. "It's blood! How on earth did that get there?"

"He must have banged his head on the way into the water," Connie said.

Eliza stood up and examined the area. "I wonder. If they're going to move the body in something as unceremonious as a wheelbarrow, it won't matter if I take a look at the back of his head first." Eliza glanced at Mr Bell. "Will you help me turn it onto its side?"

"It's a dead body. I don't want to be touching it."

"Just the shoulder, please. This might be important."

After a moment's hesitation, Mr Bell stepped forward and lifted the left shoulder of the body until the head moved.

"There it is. Connie, come and look at this."

With the same lack of enthusiasm as Mr Bell, Connie stepped forward. "It looks like someone hit him on the back of the head."

"That's my thoughts, exactly." She looked at her father. "What happened to that croquet mallet you found?"

Mr Bell studied the surroundings. "I threw it onto the bank; there it is, near the bushes. Would you say that's what they hit him with?"

Eliza retrieved the wooden implement and inspected the head. "I imagine so. If you ask me, Sir Cyril's death wasn't an accident at all, and I doubt that whoever did it expected anyone to find the body."

"You mean he was murdered?"

"That's exactly what I mean, and to be honest, it wouldn't be a surprise if he was. How many people has he upset since we arrived? And that's less than a day ago. I would say there are many people who might want him dead."

Mr Bell let out a long whistle. "That's quite an accusation... Wait, listen, is that Lord Albert coming back with the gardener? Come on, let's get out of here before they arrive. We can talk about this later."

Eliza stood up and straightened her skirt before thrusting the mallet deep into the nearest rhododendron bush. "We can come back for this later too."

The conservatory was empty when they arrived back at the house, and with his wet clothes, Mr Bell hurried on ahead. Eliza and Connie strolled into the hallway and headed for the stairs, but as Eliza put a foot on the bottom step, the door to Lord Lowton's office opened and an ashen-faced Lady Victoria rushed from the room.

"What are you looking at?" she asked as she hurried to the stairs.

"Nothing, forgive me." Eliza hesitated as she studied the woman before her. "We'd like to offer our condolences, we're sorry for what happened."

"You know?" Lady Victoria's eyes were like pinpricks as she scowled at Eliza.

"Unfortunately, we were with my father when he found the body, although I don't think anyone else knows."

"Good afternoon, my dears." Lady Caroline appeared weary as she came up behind them. "What doesn't anyone else know?"

Eliza hesitated before turning back to Lady Victoria.

"You tell her," Lady Victoria said. "I'm going for a lie down."

"What's the matter with her?" Lady Caroline said as her sister-in-law continued up the stairs.

A jumble of thoughts raced through Eliza's head as she stared at the carpet. *What do I say?*

"I'm sorry, I can't say."

"You most certainly can. Even Victoria told you to tell me."

Eliza glanced at Connie, who had distracted herself with a loose button on her coat. "I'm sorry, Caroline, but Lord Lowton told me not to say anything."

"Well, why does Victoria know? I'm sorry, Eliza, but if there's something going on, I need to be told what it is."

Eliza nodded. "Very well, but can we go somewhere more private? The library, perhaps."

A frown settled on Lady Caroline's face. "If we must, come with me."

They entered the library, but Eliza checked between the bookshelves to make sure they were alone before she told Lady Caroline to sit down.

"I'm afraid we have some rather bad news. We were out walking with Father this morning and as we approached the lake behind the formal garden, we came across a body floating in the water. The body of Sir Cyril."

Lady Caroline's eyes widened as she put a hand to her mouth. "Is he all right?"

"No. No, I'm afraid he's not. He's dead." Eliza sat beside Her Ladyship and took her hand. "Lord Lowton didn't want us to tell you because he said you already had too much to deal with today."

Lady Caroline sank back into the chair. "He's right, of course; we can't let this interfere with the ball."

Eliza and Connie exchanged a glance. "You mean you want to go ahead with it?"

Lady Caroline's eyes grew wide. "Absolutely. Have you any idea how important this ball is?"

"But your brother-in-law's dead."

"Damn fool of a fellow." Lady Caroline pushed herself up and paced the room. "Why did it have to happen today, of all days?"

"Caroline, I hardly think he did it on purpose."

"If I have to cancel tonight, everyone will be talking about it for years. Not only will Alice's life be ruined, I'll never be able to face society again. I can hear them now, laughing at my middle-class background, and their snide comments saying it isn't good enough." She turned and stared at Eliza. "Don't you see? This is my one chance to show everyone I'm as good as they are and this could finish me."

"I'm sure that's not true." Eliza stood up and took Lady Caroline's hands. "I didn't want to mention this, but what if he didn't fall? What if someone deliberately pushed him into the water?"

Lady Caroline rubbed the creases in her forehead. "You mean killed him?"

"Possibly, that's what we don't know."

Lady Caroline shook her head. "Of course he wasn't

pushed. The only people here are as good as family, who on earth would do that?"

"I don't know, but we need to call a doctor."

"Today? Don't be ridiculous. Neville's right, this has to stay between us ... at least until after the ball. Please, Eliza, don't do anything to spoil tonight. Promise me."

Lady Caroline's face softened as her eyes held Eliza's gaze. "Please."

Eliza turned away and walked towards the window. "Very well ... but only until tomorrow. We can't pretend this hasn't happened."

"No, of course not, now I must get on. Before I bumped into you I was looking for Hilda to ask her what she thought of the floral arrangements. Have you seen her?"

Seconds later, the door shut behind Lady Caroline and Eliza perched on the edge of a chair staring after her.

"Did that just happen? I told Caroline about the death of her brother-in-law, a death that could possibly be murder, and she was more concerned with the flower arrangements."

"That's how it sounded to me," Connie said. "Lady Victoria didn't sound particularly upset either."

"No, she didn't, although I think she was in shock." Eliza leaned back in the chair and closed her eyes. "I don't know, is it me? After what happened to Mrs Milwood last year, I can't help thinking that any unexplained death is a murder. I suppose it could have been an accident."

"Is that why you didn't mention the bang on the head?"

Eliza opened her eyes and turned them to the ceiling. "Probably. It didn't seem appropriate, especially after Lord Lowton told us to keep quiet. I also got the impression Lady Victoria hadn't been told about it either."

"That still wouldn't explain her lack of concern."

"No, you're right, it wouldn't." Eliza sighed. "I wish Archie was here. He'd know what to do."

"Why don't you send him a telegram and ask him to visit tomorrow?"

A smile brightened Eliza's face, and she jumped to her feet. "Yes, of course, what a splendid idea. I'll do it straight after luncheon."

CHAPTER SIX

Neither Eliza nor Connie had much of an appetite for luncheon and as soon as Lady Caroline left the dining room, they excused themselves and retired to their private sitting room.

"Have you thought about what to say in the telegram?" Connie asked as Eliza searched for a pen and some writing paper.

"Not really, I couldn't think properly with Lady Rosemary sitting beside me at the dining table, wittering on about the arrangements."

Connie took a seat near the window. "She is rather excited, but I suppose Lady Alice is her only granddaughter."

"Yes, she revels in all these formalities. That's why Caroline ended up with Lord Lowton in the first place. Ah, here we are." Eliza took some writing paper from a drawer in the writing table and sat down with her pen poised. "Now, what shall we write? How about 'Something's happened. Come at once.'?" Not waiting for Connie to reply, Eliza shook her head. "No, that won't do. How about 'Something's happened, please come at once.' Archie won't be happy having to come here on a Sunday as it is, I'd better be polite."

"Hmm. Don't you think that would get the staff talking? They'd be bound to wonder what's happened," Connie said.

"Yes, you're right. We need to make it more like an invitation. How about 'Come to Lowton soonest. Will explain once here.'?"

"Yes, that's better. Only eight words too, so it shouldn't be too expensive."

Eliza nodded. "Not as cheap as the first one, but it will do. Now, I need an envelope. There's no point making it too easy for Soams to read." Eliza opened several drawers in the desk before finding what she wanted. "While I finish off here, why don't you get your coat? We've a couple of hours to fill this afternoon, and so we may as well go back to the lake and see if we can find anything of interest."

Ten minutes later, with their hats and coats fastened, and the telegram handed to Soams, Eliza led them out of the front door.

"Why don't we go through the conservatory?" Connie asked.

"Because I don't want to meet anyone who might want to come with us. If we need to keep this whole thing quiet, it will be easier if no one sees us."

"We'd better go around to the left then. The marquee for tonight is down the right side of the house."

"Yes, I'd forgotten about that. Come on, let's hurry, we want to be back in good time for afternoon tea."

. . .

Twenty minutes later as they once again stood by the lake, Eliza surveyed the scene.

"What are we looking for?" Connie asked.

"I won't know until we find it. Perhaps we could start with the croquet mallet. We need to take it back to our rooms and keep it safe until Archie arrives." Eliza sank her arm into the bush, and when she didn't find it, she pushed her head into the foliage to take a better look.

"It's gone," she said eventually as she turned back to face Connie. "I'm sure I hid it around here, but it's disappeared."

"That's strange, who would move it?" Connie's brow creased.

"That, my dear Connie, is the question we need to answer. My guess is that whoever did knows something about Sir Cyril's death ... and may even be the killer."

"Either that or it was a member of staff."

Eliza's shoulders sagged. "Yes, there is that. Why do these people need so many servants? I'm sure it's just to confuse the likes of us."

Connie chuckled. "I'm sure it's not, but you can't deny they come in handy at a time like this."

Eliza reached into her handbag and drew out several sheets of paper and a pencil.

"What have you got there?" Connie asked.

"I thought it might be a good idea to draw the scene of the crime, so to speak." Eliza poised her pencil over the paper.

"I didn't know you could draw."

"I can't." Eliza grinned before returning her attention to the scene. "They tried, quite unsuccessfully, to teach me at school, although I must admit, I did improve at university. I needed to sketch what felt like every flower and plant known to man for my botany classes, but whether that will stand me in good stead for this, remains to be seen."

Connie remained silent as Eliza moved around the area, her pencil scratching feverishly on the paper. Ten minutes later, she stopped and held her drawing at arm's length.

"That's not bad, not for a first attempt, anyway. What do you think?"

Connie moved around to Eliza's side and studied the drawing. "What's that?"

"It's supposed to be the mallet I hid in the bushes, but I pressed on the paper too hard when I was drawing the foliage and so it's not very clear."

Connie giggled. "You've still done a better job than I would have."

"Wait a minute." Eliza's speech was slow and deliberate as she looked first to the left and then right. "How did Lords Lowton and Albert get here so quickly? These bushes are big, but they're not that big. We should have seen them coming."

Connie walked along the path to the right. "This is the way Lord Lowton left us. There's a fork in the path before the bushes end; they could have come from down there."

Eliza went to inspect the layout. "I suppose so, but what about Lord Albert? Didn't Father say he came from the left?"

"We came from the left."

"Precisely." Eliza examined the footpath. "It does veer off around the lake and so maybe he came from that direction."

"You'd still think we'd have seen him."

"You would. It's strange that both of them were so close

to the scene when Lord Lowton himself said it's a rarely visited spot."

"Look at this." Connie walked to the edge of the lake and pointed out a distinctive footprint on the water's edge.

Eliza bent down beside it and noted the dimensions on her paper. "The depth of it suggests it was made by someone carrying a bit of weight ... although the shoe size isn't very big."

"It is wide though."

"It is, and it suggests that whoever was standing here was looking out across the lake."

"Down at the body, perhaps."

"Exactly." Eliza grinned. "You know what this means, don't you? This footprint may well belong to the killer, and so we'll have to walk around looking at all the men's feet."

Connie chuckled. "As if that won't look strange. Aren't we supposed to walk as if we're carrying a book on our head at all times?" She lowered her head to study the ground as she walked towards the footpath. "I'll get a stiff neck if I walk like this for long."

Eliza rolled her eyes. "You could do it a little more subtly than that."

Connie was about to raise her head again when she pointed to the edge of the water. "What's that over there?" She bent down by the reeds. "It's a gold cufflink."

Eliza took it from her. "This looks expensive, certainly something you'd miss if you lost it."

"It's not your father's, is it?"

Eliza paused before shaking her head. "No, I don't think so. I'll show it to him to check but ... no, I'm sure it's not his."

"Could it be Lord Lowton's then?"

"It could be, but then again it could belong to any of the men who've been here this weekend."

"I don't understand it. Why would any of them push Sir Cyril into the water?" Connie peered at the spot where the body had been found.

Eliza shrugged. "From what I've seen since we arrived, I'd ask who wouldn't want to? It doesn't look as if he got along with anyone."

"Not enough to want to kill him though, surely?" Connie shuddered.

"You never know. They say you can't tell what goes on behind closed doors. If there was a family feud, they were unlikely to broadcast it."

"That's true ... and Lady Caroline certainly didn't have much time for Sir Cyril."

Eliza nodded. "You know, we might be better off back at the house. There's not much here, but the drawing room would be a perfect place to watch everyone and see if any of them look guilty. Besides, it must be nearly time for afternoon tea."

Mr Bell was reading the newspaper in the conservatory when they arrived back and he smiled when he saw them.

"I wondered where you'd got to. Have you been for another walk?"

Eliza wandered over to the door leading to the hallway and checked the surroundings before closing it and returning to the seat next to her father.

"We went back to the lake to see if we could find any more clues about Sir Cyril's death."

47

Mr Bell chuckled. "Doing your detecting again, are you? You really should leave it to the police."

"I wish I could, but neither Lord Lowton nor Caroline will let the police near the place. Not today anyway, and by the time they arrive any evidence might have disappeared."

Mr Bell stared at Eliza, his face grave. "You've told Caroline?"

"We had no choice. We saw Lady Victoria coming out of Lord Lowton's office and while we were offering our condolences, Caroline came up behind us and demanded to know what we were talking about."

Mr Bell shook his head. "You still shouldn't have said anything. Is she cancelling the ball?"

"No, that's the thing." Eliza's eyes were wide. "It was as if she thought Sir Cyril had deliberately killed himself just to inconvenience her ahead of tonight. She said Lord Lowton had been right not to say anything and that the ball must go on."

Mr Bell stared out of the window before turning back to Eliza. "I don't want you to get involved with this. There are some powerful people here, people who won't take kindly to you poking your nose into their business. You need to let Lord Lowton take charge of the situation."

"What if they try to cover it up?"

"That, I'm afraid, is their prerogative. The last thing they'll want is for this to get into the newspapers, and so they'll do whatever they can to stop it ending up in court. I really would advise you not to cause any trouble."

"But we can't let someone get away with murder, whoever they are."

"We don't know it's murder," Mr Bell said. "I expect

Lord Lowton will instruct his physician to examine the body tomorrow and they're most likely to agree that the death was accidental drowning. They'll bury him on the estate and the wider world will be none the wiser."

Eliza and Connie stared at Mr Bell.

"But they can't do that," Eliza said.

"I'm afraid that's where you're wrong. You and I can't do that, but when you make the rules, as they do, you can do as you wish ... and there's not much the likes of us can do about it."

"But Eliza's sent for Dr Thomson..."

Mr Bell scowled at Eliza. "You've not." Mr Bell stood up and walked to the window. "Ye gods, Eliza. That could change everything. If Lord Lowton agrees to him seeing the body, you must tell him to write 'drowned' on the death certificate and be done with it."

"I can't do that, he has to tell the truth. It's more than his reputation's worth."

"His reputation!" Mr Bell said. "Doctors like him don't have reputations worth saving. They're nothing but working-class butchers."

"That's not true and you know it. Archie isn't your common-or-garden surgeon, he treats patients with medicines and herbs."

"So do gypsies..."

"That's enough." Connie stood up and held her hands up between the two of them. "You shouldn't be falling out."

"No, you're right." Eliza stared down at the floor. "I'm sorry, but I thought it was for the best. I don't know for certain that Archie's coming yet, but if he does, please will you be nice to him?"

Mr Bell nodded. "If I must, but tell him not to upset Lord Lowton. He's been very hospitable to us this weekend."

"He has, but I can't promise. I may not have liked Sir Cyril, but I didn't wish him dead. We need to find whoever pushed him into the water in case they plan on killing anyone else. Besides, if we say nothing, we'd be accomplices to murder and I couldn't live with that." Eliza fidgeted with the button on her jacket as the silence grew between them.

"It must be time for afternoon tea," Connie said eventually. "I can hear voices in the hallway."

Eliza glanced at the clock on the mantelpiece. "Yes, two minutes to four. Shall we go and find a seat? We need somewhere with a good view of everyone's feet."

CHAPTER SEVEN

E liza checked her reflection in the bedroom mirror before picking up a rectangular jewellery box and carrying it to the adjoining sitting room where she knocked lightly on Connie's door.

"Are you ready?"

"Yes, I think so. Come in."

Eliza pushed on the door to find Connie in the soft lilac ballgown she had lent her. "Well, don't you look glamorous!"

"Do you think so?" Connie flushed and turned back to the mirror, smoothing her hands down the flared skirt. "I hope I can manage with the train. I'm not used to wearing them."

"I'm sure you'll be fine. I need to get used to mine as well; I've not worn this dress since we left London." Eliza flicked the back of her grey silk gown. "At least you've put on your own necklace. Would you fasten mine on for me? I usually have Archie or Iris to help."

Connie smiled and took the box from Eliza, who turned to face the mirror.

"I suppose being able to put on my own jewellery must count as a benefit of living by myself; I've no choice but to do these things. There you are."

Eliza turned back to face her.

"The sapphire in the centre sets off the dress perfectly," Connie said. "Was it a present from Archie?"

"No, Father. I thought that if he saw me wearing it tonight, he might forgive me for this afternoon."

Connie sighed. "I hope so. I hate to see the two of you not speaking to each other."

Eliza fidgeted with the box in her hand. "Let me take this back and we can go downstairs. I should imagine the other guests will be arriving by now."

Eliza was about to re-enter her bedroom when there was a knock on the outer door. She opened it with a frown on her face.

"Father. What are you doing here?"

"May I come in?" He stepped into the sitting room and waited for Eliza to close the door. "I came to apologise for being so rude about Archie. He's a good man, and he makes you happy, that's all that matters."

Eliza smiled. "Thank you, but I should apologise, too, for being angry."

"You've no need to apologise, I deserved it." He took her hand and kissed the back. "You mean the world to me, you know that?"

Before Eliza could answer, Connie joined them. "Good evening, Mr Bell. I didn't expect to see you here."

"I was beginning to wonder where you were. Most of the guests from the house have already gone over to the marquee. I've asked Rodney to save us some seats."

"Yes, we're ready. I just need to put this back in my room." Eliza waved the empty case in the air as she walked to the bedroom. "Did you notice my necklace?"

Mr Bell's eyes glistened in the light. "I did, it looks wonderful, as do you. Is that another new dress?"

"It's not very new, but it's the best I've got. I can't be too extravagant now we're out of London and I don't have so many functions to attend. I just hope nobody notices it's from last season."

"At least Lady Victoria won't be there to scrutinise you," Connie said. "I felt positively old-fashioned last night when she gave me her withering stare."

Eliza grimaced. "Yes, me too."

"Well, you both look absolutely lovely, and I won't have anyone saying anything else." Mr Bell opened the door. "Now, shall we go? The champagne will be getting warm."

Eliza and Connie both linked arms with Mr Bell as he escorted them down the stairs and towards the west door that led directly to the marquee.

"Before we go in," Eliza said, "may I ask if you've lost a cufflink while you've been here?"

Mr Bell checked the cuffs of his shirt. "No, not that I'm aware of. Why, have you found one?"

"Yes, we spotted it partially buried in the mud by the side of the lake ... close to where you pulled Sir Cyril from the water. It's a gold one."

Mr Bell shook his head. "In that case I can assure you it's not mine." He released his arm from Connie's and showed them the gold cufflinks he was wearing for the evening. "This is the only gold pair I brought with me. I had a pair of silver ones on earlier, but I put them both back in their box."

Eliza smiled. "That's a relief. I didn't think it was yours but I wanted to check. What about the croquet mallet you found? Do you know what happened to it?"

Mr Bell shrugged. "You took it from me while we were at the lake and pushed it into the bushes if I remember rightly."

"I did, but when I went back to get it, it had gone. You were the only one who knew I'd put it there, so I wondered if you'd moved it."

"No, it wasn't me. I've not left the house since we got back this morning."

"Who could have moved it then? I made sure the mallet wasn't visible from the path, and so whoever took it knew what they were looking for."

"You mean they wanted it to disappear?" Mr Bell raised an eyebrow at his daughter.

"That's exactly what I mean. I wonder if we could suggest a game of croquet tomorrow morning and check the mallets they give us."

"That would be splendid," Connie said. "I don't think I've played croquet since I used to visit you in the big house in Moreton. I did enjoy it too."

"You can count me out," Mr Bell said. "I don't want to get involved with any of this, thank you very much."

Eliza took a deep breath. "Let's not start that again; I'll speak to Caroline about it over breakfast."

Once they reached the marquee, Mr Bell pointed to a table towards the back of the room occupied by Sir Rodney and Lady Rosemary. "There they are, follow me."

They navigated their way around an array of tables and as they arrived, Mr Bell accepted three glasses of champagne from a waitress.

"I was beginning to think you'd got lost," Sir Rodney said as they sat down.

"I'm sorry, it was my fault," Eliza said. "I kept him talking outside. Have we missed anything?"

"Only the first quadrille and a polka," Lady Rosemary said. "There are plenty more to go. I saved you both a dance card in case you wish to join in."

Eliza smirked at Connie. "Maybe later. Who was the lucky man to have the first dance with Lady Alice?"

Lady Rosemary smiled. "It was quite a family affair, actually. She paired up with Lord David and Lady Mary, Sir Cyril's son and daughter, and Henry made up the foursome."

Eliza paused, her champagne glass halfway to her lips. "Sir Cyril's son and daughter are here?"

"Well naturally, just because their father's ill is no reason for them to miss out. Lady Victoria brought them. She's sitting over at the other side of the marquee with the Forsyths and Beauforts, amongst others."

Eliza took a large gulp of her champagne.

"Lady Victoria's here?" Connie sounded as shocked as Eliza felt.

"Naturally. She wouldn't want to miss out ... or more to the point, she wouldn't want to miss the chance of being photographed at one of the first coming-out balls of the season. She had the first dance with Caroline and Lord Lowton to make sure the photographer saw her."

Eliza peered across the room to see the attractive blonde in a daring gown holding court amongst a crowd of equally glamorous guests.

"Who was her partner for the dance?" Eliza struggled to keep the tone of her voice level.

"Not anyone I know, if I'm being honest," Lady Rosemary said. "I heard someone say he worked on the estate, the estate manager, I think. I wouldn't have thought she'd mix with his type, but they seemed to get along well enough."

"Don't they just." Eliza watched as Lady Victoria flirted with a broad-shouldered man with an olive complexion and a pencil moustache. *Certainly not the behaviour I would expect from someone who's just lost her husband.*

"Well, she doesn't seem to be missing Sir Cyril," Eliza said as Lady Victoria headed towards the dance floor, her hand resting on the arm of the estate manager.

"I'm sure she's glad for an evening without him," Lady Rosemary said. "I think she has far more fun when he's not around."

Eliza and Connie exchanged glances. "Did ... do you know Sir Cyril well?"

Lady Rosemary feigned a sniff and pulled back her shoulders. "Well enough, don't we, Rodney?"

"What's that, m'dear?" Sir Rodney turned away from Mr Bell.

"Eliza was just asking about Sir Cyril. You've had your fair share of problems with him, haven't you?"

"That I have."

"What sort of problems?"

"Problems that come from being in the company of a snob. Most of the family were very welcoming when Caroline first met Neville, but not him. You always knew he was looking down his nose at you and in those early days I couldn't hold my tongue."

"Did it make him change?" Connie asked.

Sir Rodney laughed. "Not in the slightest; if anything it made him worse ... and he's never stopped. The last time we had words was when I got my knighthood. Neville held a small party in my honour after the ceremony at the Palace. A very nice affair it was, too, but if I'm honest, it would have been a lot better if Sir Cyril hadn't been there. He accused me of abusing Neville's position and said that Her Majesty shouldn't be giving honours to men like me."

"What a horrible thing to say," Connie said.

"Well, exactly," Lady Rosemary said. "He was even offhand with me last night when I had the misfortune to sit next to him for dinner. I specifically said to Caroline, *'Caroline, please don't sit me next to your brother-in-law'*, but did she pay any attention? No, she did not ... and then we had the commotion in the hallway with Henry. After that, Caroline told Neville she didn't want Sir Cyril here tonight. I've no idea what Neville said to him, but it seemed to do the trick."

It certainly did. Eliza bit down on her lip.

"At least he spoke to you," Connie said. "He sat next to me all through dinner and barely acknowledged me."

"That was because you had me watching over you." Mr Bell winked at Connie.

"And you should be very grateful," Lady Rosemary said. "The worst thing is his attitude is rubbing off on his son. Lord David used to be a lovely child but of late he's become so rude. I'm surprised he's getting along so well with Henry."

Eliza scanned the room looking for her son and smiled when she saw him attempting a waltz with Lady Alice.

"They seem to be getting along very well." Eliza nodded in the pair's direction and all eyes followed hers. A moment later, she saw Lord Lowton striding across the room towards them.

"Good evening, Neville," Lady Rosemary said. "Have you come to join us?"

Lord Lowton stopped and surveyed the group. "No, actually I haven't. I wanted a word with Mr Bell. Could you excuse us?"

Mr Bell shrugged as he left the table and followed His Lordship outside. He returned a little over a minute later, his face red.

"What's the matter?" Eliza asked when he didn't sit down.

"I need to speak to Henry. I'll wait until the music stops so as not to cause a scene."

"Why do you need to speak to Henry?" Eliza was on her feet standing beside her father. "Is that what Lord Lowton wanted to talk to you about?"

Mr Bell sighed. "He reminded me that the purpose of the ball was to find a suitable husband for Lady Alice..."

"And he doesn't see Henry as suitable?"

Mr Bell's eyes didn't leave the dance floor as he watched his grandson glide around the dance floor. "No, he doesn't. He said that if I don't put a stop to it immediately, I can say goodbye to my knighthood."

"He blackmailed you?" Eliza's eyes were wide.

"It's not really blackmail, but yes, well, I suppose he did. You can see his point of view though. Henry's only in his second year at Cambridge and if he trains to be a doctor, it will be years before he's ready to marry anyone."

"I don't imagine the Lowtons will want to wait that long

for Lady Alice to be settled, even if they do consider Henry suitable, which they don't."

"No, you're right," Mr Bell said. "They're probably hoping she'll marry the eldest son of someone with a title."

"And there was me thinking it was only Sir Cyril who was like that. It looks as if they're all as bad as each other." Eliza helped herself to two more glasses of champagne as a waitress glided past, and handed one to Connie.

"This is rather nice, don't you think? I feel as if I'm floating." Connie giggled as she accepted the glass.

Eliza laughed. "No more after this, then."

"Mrs Thomson, may I disturb you?" Soams stood next to her, his demeanour as formal as ever. "A telegram for you."

"My, that's late for a Saturday evening. Thank you, I don't expect I'll need to reply."

Soams gave a slight bow and backed away. "Very good, madam."

"What's that?" Mr Bell looked over his daughter's shoulder and she undid the envelope.

"It's from Archie. He's coming to join us tomorrow." Eliza grinned at Connie but the smile faded as she turned to Mr Bell. "You haven't forgotten you promised to be nice to him, have you?"

Mr Bell nodded. "No, I've not, but don't forget what I told you about playing detective. Are you listening?"

Eliza's nod was less than enthusiastic.

"Do you think you ought to tell Lord Lowton or Lady Caroline he's coming?" Connie asked.

"I suppose I should, although they're both rather preoccupied at the moment."

"Well, don't put it off," Mr Bell said. "I know you, if you don't want to do something you'll wait until it's too late. Come on, we've got a minute now, between dances. I'll have a word with Henry, and you can speak to Lord Lowton at the same time."

Before Eliza had time to object, Mr Bell had taken her by the arm and led her onto the dance floor.

"Good evening, Mrs Thomson." His Lordship frowned as Mr Bell unlinked his arm and left her standing immediately in front of him. "Would you care to dance?"

"N-no, no thank you. I'm afraid I'm not familiar with the Schottische. No, I came to tell you, and I hope it will be helpful to you, that my husband, Dr Thomson, has agreed to join us tomorrow." She lowered her voice. "I wondered if he might certify the body for you, to save you from calling anyone else out. He'll be very discreet."

Lord Lowton glared at her. "You've told him? You had no right."

"I'm sorry, but you can't pretend nothing's happened."

"I can do what I like on my estate." Lord Lowton's voice rose as the orchestra sounded the opening bars of the next song, forcing him to escort her to the edge of the dance floor. "I don't want the police involved."

"Why would they be?" Eliza raised an eyebrow at His Lordship.

"Because news around here travels fast and if it gets in the newspapers, they'll be swarming around here like bees around a honey jar. In case you're not aware, the death of an honourable gentleman will arouse a great deal of curiosity and if any of this becomes public knowledge, I will hold you personally responsible."

CHAPTER EIGHT

B y the time Eliza returned to her room that night, there was a note on letterheaded paper resting on the corner of the bed. She picked it up and immediately hurried back into the sitting room where she almost collided with Connie, who was coming out of her own bedroom.

"Have you got a letter?" Connie asked.

"I have." Eliza read out the text. "Dear Guest. Please be advised that breakfast will be served at nine o'clock tomorrow morning. We request that you join us promptly as we have some news we wish to share. Please do not disturb Lady Caroline or myself this evening as we will provide no further details at this time. Yours faithfully, Neville, The Earl of Lowton."

"Yes, mine says the same. Do you think they'll tell everyone about Sir Cyril?"

"I would imagine so, although how they'll get around the fact that the man will have been dead for almost a day by the time he tells them, I've no idea."

Connie shuddered. "We didn't get much of a breakfast

this morning with Sir Cyril causing such a fuss. It doesn't look like we'll get much tomorrow either."

Eliza glanced at the clock on the mantelpiece. "It's turned midnight now too. I suggest we try to get some sleep and arrive for breakfast a little early to make sure we get a good seat."

By the time they arrived in the breakfast room the following morning, most of the guests had already arrived.

"What do you think it could be about?" Eliza heard Lady Beaufort ask Lady Rosemary.

"I'm sure I've no idea. Caroline hasn't told me, whatever it is."

"It looks like the only people not here are Lord Lowton and Lady Caroline," Eliza said as Connie helped herself to a sausage and two softly poached eggs.

"Do you blame them? After a note like that everyone was bound to be here early. I imagine they'll arrive on the dot of nine o'clock."

Eliza filled her own plate before heading towards the two empty chairs Mr Bell had reserved for them.

"It will be interesting to watch everyone's reactions when the news is broken," Mr Bell said. "Whoever did it is bound to feel uncomfortable in a room as full as this. Look, even Henry's here." He waved over to his grandson, who acknowledged him but went to get himself a plate of food.

"What time's Archie arriving?" Mr Bell asked.

"He didn't say, but I imagine it will be at least eleven o'clock. He'll be coming in the carriage with it being a Sunday and so it will take him a while to get here."

"Do you think we'll be expected to go to church?" Connie asked.

"I hope not." Eliza kept her voice low. "We've got a killer to catch, we haven't got time to sit around doing nothing."

Connie tutted. "Eliza Thomson, you'd better watch yourself. Kneeling down to pray is hardly a waste of time."

Eliza smiled at Connie. *If you say so.*

The clock struck nine as the double doors at the far end of the room opened and Lord Lowton, wearing a sombre expression and a black armband, walked into the room. In case anyone missed the subtleties of his mourning, Lady Caroline followed him dressed from head to toe in black.

"Oh my goodness."

"Who's died?"

"What's going on?"

The questions became distorted as the guests rose to their feet and Lord Lowton strode to the head of the table and raised his hands to demand silence.

"Please, everyone. Take your seats, I'll explain everything."

His request didn't silence the murmurings, but once everyone returned to their seats, he gave a small cough to clear his throat.

"It's with deep regret that I stand here today to report that the body of my beloved brother, the Honourable Cyril Lowton, has been found drowned in the lake at the back of the formal garden."

Gasps came from around the table, the most noticeable from Lady Hilda. "Cyril's dead? He can't be." She fumbled in her bag for a handkerchief.

"I say, old man, what happened?" Lord Forsyth put an arm around his wife's shoulders.

"It's a good question, but one I'm unable to answer, I'm afraid. We believe that the most likely explanation is that he slipped and fell into the water. We have a doctor calling this morning who should be able to confirm the details and certify the death. In the meantime, I would ask you not to share the news with anyone outside this room. We all know how the press like to get hold of a story and twist it for their own ends, and I don't want my brother's death to be a source of their speculation."

"They'll get nothing out of me," Lord Forsyth said.

"Nor me," Lord Beaufort added. "I've had enough run-ins with them over the years to know when to keep my head down."

"You will put an obituary in *The Times*, won't you?" Lady Hilda said. "We must do the right thing ... and arrange a proper funeral."

Lord Lowton nodded. "Of course, we'll do everything as we should, but I'd like to keep the details quiet until we've made the arrangements."

"When did you find him?"

Eliza turned to the far end of the table and saw Sir Rodney on his feet.

"Find him ... you mean Cyril?"

"Yes, when was his body discovered ... and who found it? It would have been pitch black at the lake by the time the ball ended last night. Did you know about it while the ball was still going on?"

Eliza turned back to the other end of the table and for a second her eyes met Lord Lowton's.

"Yes, actually I did, but by the time we found his body, it was too late to cancel on our guests. Cyril would have understood, he wouldn't have wanted Lady Alice to miss her ball."

"Have you told Alice?" Lady Hilda asked.

"Not yet." Lord Lowton pursed his lips. "She was still sleeping when we came down. Caroline will tell her later."

"How's Lady Victoria?" Lady Beaufort asked. "She must be devastated. She had a lovely evening last night too. How awful it must have been to come back to the house to find Sir Cyril ... you know."

"Yes, she is rather upset," Lord Lowton said. "We told the children this morning and they've stayed with her. It's rather fortunate they're staying here and hadn't gone back to the cottage. I'll ask the doctor to look in on her when he arrives."

Lady Caroline stepped forward and whispered into her husband's ear.

"Ah yes, I nearly forgot. Caroline would like to remind you that despite the news, you are all most welcome to stay for the rest of the day as planned and to take Sunday luncheon with us. Cook has the meat already in the oven, and so if you leave before we eat, we'll have rather a lot left over. Please feel free to use the facilities between now and one o'clock."

The murmuring around the table increased as Lord and Lady Lowton withdrew from the room, and as the door closed behind them, Mr Bell leaned over to talk to Eliza and Connie.

"They all look suitably upset. Who do you think did it?"

Eliza put a finger to her lips. "Be quiet, they'll hear you."

"Perhaps we should finish off here and go for that game of croquet," Connie said. "We'll be able to talk out there."

Eliza nodded before she spotted Henry strolling towards them from the back of the room. She leaned across her father as he took the empty seat next to Mr Bell.

"What's the matter with you? You look terrible."

Henry's skin was pale against the deep brown of his eyes. "Nothing, I just didn't get much sleep last night."

"Well, we're going for a game of croquet on the back lawn. Would you care to join us if you're on your own?"

"I'm not on my own."

"Oh." Eliza exaggerated her glance around the room. "I don't see any of your friends here."

"Albert will be down shortly."

"As long as it's him and not Lady Alice you're waiting for. Grandfather told you last night how Lord Lowton feels about you spending too much time with her."

Henry gritted his teeth. "We're only friends, I'm not going to marry her."

"I know you're not, but last night was a time for Lady Alice to find herself a husband ... in fact the whole of this season is. She can hardly do that with you as her constant companion."

Henry picked up a piece of toast and stood up. "I'll see you later."

Eliza watched Henry leave the room and then without a word followed him into the hall. Once she was sure he had gone, she made her way up the stairs, relieved that Connie was behind her. She said nothing until they were alone in their sitting room.

"There are times I wish Archie had been firmer with that

boy. I don't know what I've done to upset him, but I'd like to give him a thick ear."

"He's all right. I suppose he's just upset about being told to stay away from Lady Alice."

Eliza sighed. "Perhaps you're right, although he's been very distant since we moved to Moreton and I don't know why."

"I imagine he preferred it when you lived in London."

"I'm sure he did, but is that a reason to stay away? The only time he comes home is when he needs more money. I must get Archie to have a word with him. Anyway, enough of him, let me get my coat and we can go into the garden."

With their hats and coats fastened they walked back to the hall, but hadn't reached the door to the conservatory when there was a knock on the front door and Soams ushered Archie in.

Eliza beamed at him. "My, you're nice and early. I wasn't expecting you for another hour."

"I've got to be back for four o'clock and so I thought I'd make an early start. What's this all about?"

"We need to find Lord Lowton but I need to talk to you first." Eliza glanced around the hallway. "We'd better go somewhere quiet."

"Why don't we go up to our sitting room?" Connie asked. "I imagine all the rooms down here will be busy."

"You have your own sitting room?" Archie's eyebrows rose. "You've piqued my curiosity now. I must see this."

CHAPTER NINE

Archie stepped into the sitting room and let out a long whistle.

"Very nice. What did you do to get this?"

"I was the guest of honour on Friday night, I'll have you know." Eliza giggled. "I had to lead the procession into the dining room with Lord Lowton."

"The guest of honour!"

"It was only because all the other guests around the table were related and so they didn't count." Eliza's face straightened. "Anyway, I don't think I'm the most popular person here any more, not after yesterday."

"What have you done?"

"I've not done anything, but we found a dead body yesterday morning, the earl's younger brother. With so many guests being here for the ball, Lord Lowton didn't want to call a doctor, but the death needs certifying. The trouble is, I wrote to you without telling him."

Archie shook his head. "Why did you do that? There must be a local doctor he could have called on instead of getting me all the way up here."

"There may be, but there's a complication."

Archie looked skyward. "Don't tell me, you think someone murdered him."

"Don't say it like that."

"You do, don't you? Eliza, just because you find a dead body, doesn't mean someone murdered them."

"I know that, but I was right last time about Mrs Milwood and there's something about this that feels wrong." Eliza told him of the damage to the back of Sir Cyril's head.

"He could have banged it when he fell into the water."

"He could have, but there was a croquet mallet smeared with blood near the scene. It just looks suspicious ... and I wanted you to come and see for yourself."

"So does Lord Lowton know I'm here?"

"Yes, he does, but he wants you to certify that Sir Cyril drowned."

Archie studied his wife before turning to Connie.

Connie nodded. "It's true. Lord Lowton's telling everyone it was an accident."

Archie sighed. "All right then, let's go and find him and ask if I can examine the body."

Eliza and Connie took Archie back downstairs and thankfully found Soams in the hallway.

"Could you tell us where His Lordship is?" Eliza asked.

Soams nodded and beckoned them to follow him. He knocked on the office door before letting himself in.

"Mrs Thomson, Mrs Appleton and their guest to see you, sir."

At the sight of Archie, Lord Lowton stood up.

"This is my husband Dr Thomson," Eliza said as Archie held out his hand to their host.

"Good morning, Dr Thomson. Thank you for coming. Has your wife filled you in on the details?"

"Yes sir, she has. Would I be able to examine the body?"

"Yes, of course. We placed it in a folly beyond the lake and so it will take about half an hour to walk there."

"I don't mind that," Archie said. "I've been sitting in a carriage for the last two hours, it will be good to stretch my legs."

Lord Lowton scowled at Eliza and Connie as they stood with their hats and coats on. "It might be too far for the ladies to walk."

"No, it sounds delightful." Eliza conjured up her best smile. "Fortunately, we both have our sturdy walking boots with us."

Lord Lowton hesitated. "Yes, right, well let me lead the way."

As predicted it was half an hour later before they arrived at the folly and Lord Lowton took the keys from his pocket and unlocked the door.

"Here we are, Doctor, I'm sure you'll find it was a simple drowning. If we could get the death certificate, then I can alert the relevant authorities." Lord Lowton held the door for them but didn't follow them inside. "If you don't mind, I'll wait out here. I'd rather not see my dear brother in such a state again."

Archie nodded and watched as Lord Lowton walked to a stone bench about ten yards away.

"Look here." Eliza held Sir Cyril's head off the ground. "Don't tell me that's been made by the edge of a muddy lake. I'd say it's the imprint of a croquet mallet."

Archie crouched down and examined the wound. "I can't deny it does. It looks as if the impact came from low down. Do you have the mallet to hand?"

"No, that's the thing. I hid it in some bushes for safekeeping but when we went back for it, it had disappeared. When you arrived we were about to go for a game of croquet to check the mallets they have out on the lawn."

Archie sighed and continued to examine the rest of the body. He paused moments later as Eliza crouched on the floor beside him, her pencil and paper in hand.

"What are you doing?"

"I've not told you yet but there was a footprint in the mud near the place we found the body. I want to measure the size of Sir Cyril's foot while I have the chance and then compare it with the one we found, just to make sure it's not his." Eliza held the paper against Sir Cyril's right shoe and attempted to draw an outline. "There, that should be good enough. I already have a sketch of the footprint, but hopefully the real thing will still be there and I can measure it precisely against this." She admired her handiwork and put the paper back in her bag as Archie shook his head.

"You said your father found the body. Do you know if it was floating?"

Eliza's forehead creased. "I didn't think to ask him. He was trying to pull it from the water when we arrived."

"So the water wasn't deep?"

"I would say it's not deep enough for a grown man to drown in. You need to come and look."

Archie stood up and towered over the body, his hands on his hips. "I can't sign the death certificate as it is. I can't say for certain whether the cause of death was drowning or the blow to the back of the head but my suspicion is that it was the blow."

"So he was dead when he hit the water?"

"Looking at the severity of the head wound I would say so, but even if he wasn't, the blow would have knocked him unconscious so he wouldn't have been able to save himself when he hit the water. If your father can confirm the body was floating that would be enough to suggest a murder ... for the time being at least."

"Why?" Connie couldn't keep the puzzlement from her face.

Archie smiled at her. "When someone drowns, the lungs fill with water and then because there is no air in the body, it sinks. On the other hand, if the person is dead before they hit the water, they still have air in their lungs and so they float. At least in the short term."

"And so Mr Bell could tell us whether it was an accident or murder?"

"There will always be some doubt, which is why we'll need a post-mortem, but yes, essentially he could."

Eliza took a deep breath. "Will you tell Lord Lowton?"

"I don't have much choice, do I?" Archie walked to the door and held it open before leading the way to Lord Lowton.

"Is it done?" Lord Lowton asked.

Archie studied his shoes before he spoke. "Unfortunately not. The thing is, I can't be certain of the cause of death."

"Call yourself a doctor?" Lord Lowton gaped at Archie. "The man clearly drowned, can't you see that?"

"So it would appear to the untrained eye." Archie kept his eyes fixed on Lord Lowton's. "Unfortunately, I noticed a rather large gash in the back of the head which appears consistent with the croquet mallet I understand was near the body when you found it."

"A gash?"

"Yes sir, and I believe that when we get back to the house a piece of evidence from Mr Bell will confirm that someone murdered your brother."

"Murdered? But that's preposterous."

"Yes sir, I'm sure it must seem quite irregular, but it means we'll need a post-mortem and inquest to confirm the findings before I can sign the death certificate."

The colour drained from Lord Lowton's face. "You can't call the coroner today, it's Sunday for heaven's sake. And what are we supposed to do with the body while we wait?"

"I don't think we have any choice. The body has been dead for approximately twenty-four hours and the coroner really should have been called yesterday. If you don't report it today, it could land you in trouble."

"Have you any idea who you're talking to, Dr Thomson? I don't take orders from the likes of you."

Eliza stepped forward. "Forgive me for interrupting, but perhaps you could consult Lord Beaufort." Seeing Archie's forehead furrow, she continued. "He's a law lord who's staying here for the weekend."

Archie nodded. "That would do for now, but given that

the circumstances of the death are suspicious I'm sure he'll confirm we need a post-mortem."

Lord Lowton rubbed his left eye as it twitched. "I'm really not sure this is necessary."

Archie pulled himself up to his full height and looked down at His Lordship. "With respect, sir, if someone murdered your brother, I presume you'd like to find his killer."

"Yes, yes, you're right, of course. Let me go and speak to Beaufort and see what he has to say." He turned to walk away, but hadn't gone more than half a dozen steps when he stopped and turned back to face them. "Aren't you coming?"

"If you don't mind, I'd like to take a look at the place you found the body," Archie said. "The ladies can show me where it is, you go on ahead and we'll catch you up."

CHAPTER TEN

W ith Lord Lowton's squat figure fading into the distance, Eliza linked her arm through Archie's.

"Well done, he wouldn't have taken that from me. Shall we go and see the scene of the crime?"

Archie's eyes glinted as he smiled. "I imagine saying no isn't an answer I'd get away with."

Eliza grinned. "You know me so well."

They set off for the other side of the lake and by the time they arrived, fifteen minutes later, the sun was warm. Eliza immediately showed Archie the print they had found.

"What do you think? It's not very big, but given the depth in the mud, I would say a heavy man with small feet made it." She reached in her bag and took out her papers before laying the new sketch on the ground alongside the footprint. "I thought so, Sir Cyril didn't make this print, his feet were too big."

Archie nodded. "So it would seem. We don't know about the overall build of the man who made it though. If the mud was soft, it could belong to someone quite slender."

"We wondered that," Connie said. "That's why we've been studying the feet of all the men staying at the hall."

"You've been studying men's feet? And have you come to any conclusions?"

Connie's face flushed as Archie stared at her. "Only that it's not easy to work out who did this when they all seem to have small feet."

"And that we need to come up with another way to study them if I'm to base my suspicions on a footprint," Eliza added.

"Well, as long as you don't go around stealing everyone's shoes…" Archie's laugh ended abruptly. "Eliza, I wasn't being serious."

"You may not have been, but you're right. Why didn't I think of it earlier? I need to check all the shoes against my sketch." She studied the paper again. "Is this drawing accurate enough? Perhaps I should do it again to be sure."

Fifteen minutes later, with a new sketch in her bag and the rest of the scene once again scoured for clues, Eliza put her arm through Archie's as they headed back to the house. "I would say it's time for a sherry."

The guests were gathering in the drawing room by the time they returned to the house and Soams announced them as they entered the room. Lady Caroline immediately hurried towards them.

"Archie, dear." She held out a hand for him to kiss. "It's been far too long. Why on earth did you become an English country doctor when you had the world at your feet in London?"

Archie laughed. "Because my feet were getting tired. How do you enjoy being the lady of the manor? This is a change from the high life of London."

Lady Caroline put the back of a hand to her forehead. "It's just so stressful. You have no idea how much planning went into the ball last night ... and then you didn't attend. We missed you." She leaned forward with a conspiratorial look. "I presume Eliza's told you about poor old Cyril."

"She has, that's why I'm here. I've just come back from examining the body."

This time Lady Caroline's flinch wasn't for effect. "Oh my goodness, how could you? What a terrible thing to do for a living."

Archie shrugged. "Someone has to, I suppose."

"And was Neville right ... that he drowned?"

"Erm, actually, no..."

"I think we'd better wait for Lord Lowton to tell us." Eliza nodded towards the door as she saw His Lordship enter the room with Lord Beaufort.

Lady Caroline waved them over. "Darling, over here. Archie here was just telling me he's been to examine the body, but he won't tell me what he found."

Lady Caroline's pout caused Eliza to roll her eyes at Connie.

"I didn't think you'd want me to tell anyone, until you'd spoken to your friend the law lord," Archie said.

Lord Lowton ushered them to a corner of the room away from the rest of the guests. "Dr Thomson, this is Lord Beaufort; Beaufort, this is the chap Thomson I was telling you about."

Lord Beaufort offered Archie his hand. "Is it now? You're

the one who said we need to involve the coroner and have a post-mortem?"

"Yes, sir. As I explained to His Lordship, I believe the most likely cause of death was a blow to the back of the head. The fact the body ended up in the lake was a sheer circumstance of where the attack took place."

"Murder!" Lady Caroline's eyes were wide. "Who would do such a thing?"

"Quiet, Caroline." Lord Lowton scowled at his wife before glancing around the room to check nobody had noticed. "That's obviously something we need to find out."

"I'd just like to confirm my suspicions with Mr Bell before we do anything," Archie said.

"Yes, of course." Lord Lowton gave a slight cough. "I've spoken with my learned friend here and on the assumption you're right, we've decided it would best to get the whole thing over and done with as soon as possible. Lord Beaufort has kindly agreed to lead the investigation while all the guests are still here."

"How splendid." Lady Caroline clapped her hands in front of her chest. "It's like a real-life murder mystery."

"It will be no such thing. Once luncheon's over, Beaufort will take a statement from each guest to determine who the murderer is before everyone goes home."

Eliza nearly choked on the mouthful of sherry she had just taken. "You won't solve a murder investigation with just one round of statements."

Lord Lowton glared at her. "May I remind you, madam, that Lord Beaufort has one of the finest legal minds in the country?"

"But the murderer isn't just going to admit to the crime …

you need evidence. Don't you think you should call in the police?"

The colour in Lord Lowton's cheeks rose. "I told you last night I don't want the police involved. It would do nothing but bring scandal upon us, and I'm sure the villagers don't want their daily lives disturbed by the men from Fleet Street when they find out. I'll announce our intentions before luncheon and I don't want to hear any more about the police. Is that clear?"

Lord Lowton turned on his heel and left with Lord Beaufort following in his wake.

"The way Lord Lowton talks you'd think finding a murderer was easy," Eliza said.

"It's all very exciting though, don't you think?" Lady Caroline said. "Didn't you solve a murder for the police last year?"

"I did, but it's not as simple as it sounds. Once we started asking questions it took weeks to work through the lies and half-truths to find out who did it."

"What a shame you can't sit in with Lord Beaufort when he conducts the interviews," Lady Caroline said. "You might have been able to help."

Eliza stifled a laugh. "You know as well as I do that Lord Beaufort would never agree to that, despite how much I may like to."

"You're right of course. What else could we do?"

Eliza paused and stared at Archie until he became restless under her gaze.

"Don't look at me."

"But you'd be perfect," Eliza said. "You're a doctor, you're familiar with the injury and the supposed cause of death. How could he say no to having someone like you sitting in on the questioning?"

Archie shook his head. "I don't know..."

"Of course, what a marvellous idea." With a glint in her eye, Lady Caroline put a hand on Eliza's arm. "Leave it with me, I'll see what I can do."

Eliza watched as Lady Caroline made for the door, before she spotted her father entering the room. His face lit up when he saw her, but the smile quickly faded when he noticed Archie.

"Don't be like that," Eliza said as she walked over to meet him. "You promised you'd be nice to him, besides, Archie would like a word with you."

"Me? Why?"

"He has a question for you."

"Mr Bell." Archie's tone was brusque as he held out his hand to his father-in-law.

"Archibald. I didn't expect to see you this weekend."

"Well, no. I hadn't planned on coming, but Eliza told me about the incident."

"Yes, terrible affair."

"Stop beating about the bush," Eliza said to Archie. "You wanted to ask Father about the body."

"Yes, right." Archie lowered his voice. "Mr Bell, when you found the body, do you remember if it was floating on the surface of the water?"

"Of course it was floating, if it hadn't been I wouldn't have seen it, would I?"

Archie took a deep breath. "No, of course you wouldn't. I just needed to check."

"Is that it?" Mr Bell said.

"Yes, for now. If you'll excuse me, I must find Lord Lowton."

Archie hadn't reached the door before Eliza rounded on him. "Did you have to be so abrupt?"

"Well, what a stupid question."

"That's beside the point. The fact the body was floating confirms this is a murder investigation and so we had to be sure. I hope you'll apologise when he gets back."

Mr Bell took a glass of sherry from a passing maid. "Why's it all my fault? If he'd said that in the first place..." Mr Bell stopped as Eliza glared at him. "All right, if it keeps you happy."

As the clock struck one o'clock, a gong sounded in the hall and the group made their way to the dining room. When they arrived, Lord Lowton was already standing by his seat at the head of the table. He indicated for everyone to sit down before he cleared his throat and held up his hands for silence.

"Before we begin, I've an announcement. I told you this morning that the body of Sir Cyril was found yesterday in the lake behind the formal gardens. We initially assumed he had drowned after accidentally falling into the water. Since then, however, we've been joined by Dr Thomson." His Lordship paused and gestured towards Archie. "Unfortunately, he's come to the conclusion that rather than being an accident, the death was in fact murder."

"Murder!" The word reverberated around the table several times and Lord Lowton paused until the noise died down. "As you can imagine, we need to find the person who would do such a thing, and so my good friend Lord Beaufort has agreed to interview everyone who was in the house on Saturday morning. In addition, as he's familiar with the details of the injuries, Dr Thomson will sit in on the questioning, should there be any need for clarification of the matter."

Archie shifted in his seat as all eyes turned to him. "Now look what you've done," he whispered to Eliza.

"I should think so. I need to know what goes on in those interviews and so I expect a full report when they're over. Can I trust you to do that ... and ask any questions that Lord Beaufort may overlook?"

"I can't interfere."

"Of course you can, if you think Lord Beaufort's missed anything."

"What time do we need an alibi for?" Lady Rosemary asked to no one in particular.

"I would say for between ten and eleven o'clock," Eliza said. "The body was found at about half past ten."

"On Saturday morning?" Sir Rodney said. "You kept that quiet for long enough."

"We only did what we had to, Father," Lady Caroline said. "We couldn't cancel the ball."

"I've no idea what I was doing then," Lady Hilda said. "Somebody here must be able to vouch for me."

"Well, I was in the marquee with Caroline, helping with the preparations," Lady Rosemary said.

"Weren't you with Victoria?" Lord Forsyth said to Lady Hilda.

"Yes, I was, well remembered." She turned to Lord Beaufort. "Will you interview her, with her being the widow?"

"Only if she's up to it."

Lady Hilda stood up. "I must go upstairs and remind her

we were together, just in case she is. We need to get our stories straight."

"I was with you if you remember?" Lady Beaufort added.

The confused expression in Lady Hilda's eyes quickly disappeared. "Of course you were, dear. The more of us the better."

"Fortunately, I have two people to vouch for me." Mr Bell winked at his daughter. "I was out walking with Eliza and Mrs Appleton."

"Weren't you the one who found the body?" Lord Forsyth asked. "You're weren't with the ladies at the time, I hope."

"No, of course not ... but I'd only left them a couple of minutes earlier. I wouldn't have had time to kill anyone."

Lord Beaufort snorted. "How long does it take to hit someone over the head? You may need to refine your alibi, Mr Bell. Can you account for every minute between leaving your daughter and His Lordship hearing your call? I'll need to consider the evidence very carefully."

"You can't believe my father had anything to do with this before you've even spoken to anyone?" Eliza's voice squeaked as she spoke.

"I'm just warning him to be prepared." Lord Beaufort spread a napkin on his knee. "Somebody here must be short of an alibi."

CHAPTER ELEVEN

With luncheon over, Eliza and Connie made their way to the conservatory to wait with the rest of the guests for Soams to call their names.

"You don't suppose Lord Beaufort believes your father is the murderer, do you?" Connie asked.

"I would hope not because he's wrong if he thinks he is. For someone who's made it to the House of Lords, he should have more brains than that."

"So what do we say happened when your father left us?"

"We tell him the truth. We followed close behind him towards the bushes and heard him calling out not long after. We can't have been separated for more than a minute or two."

"Do you think that will be enough?"

Eliza stood up to refill her coffee cup. "I would hope so. Besides, why would Father want to kill Sir Cyril? He had no motive; in fact, he hardly knew him."

Connie nodded. "Yes, that's a good point. Nobody was talking about motives over luncheon, but you've always said you need opportunity and motive. Do you think Lord Beaufort will ask us that?"

"I would imagine so; he must be well practised in this sort of thing."

Eliza didn't have long to wait before Soams walked into the conservatory and called her name.

"Good afternoon, Mrs Thomson." Lord Beaufort gestured towards a chair opposite him when she joined him in the library. Eliza smiled at Archie as she sat down. "Now, from what I've heard already, you were walking in the formal garden with Mr Bell and Mrs Appleton shortly before Mr Bell found the body of Sir Cyril. Can you tell us what happened between the time your father left you and the time he called out to say he'd found the body in the water, several minutes later?"

Eliza gave Lord Beaufort her best smile. "Yes, of course. We were walking down the left-hand path of the garden when Father saw Sir Cyril near the rhododendron bushes that divide the garden from the lake. He wanted a quick word with him and so he took the path to the right. We followed, but at a slower pace, and saw Sir Cyril disappear behind the bushes when Father was still a good hundred feet from him. Within a minute or so, Father had disappeared as well, but seconds later we heard him calling out. We hurried along the path where we found him with Lord Lowton and Lord Albert trying to pull the body from the water."

"And so there was probably at least a minute or more where you lost sight of Mr Bell?"

"Well, yes, but as I said, by the time we arrived Lords Lowton and Albert were with him and so he wasn't on his own for more than a few seconds."

Lord Beaufort peered at Eliza. "As I understand it, Lord Lowton and Lord Albert only arrived in response to Mr Bell's calls moments before you did."

"Which suggests that Father called for help as soon as he saw the body. Why would he even want to hurt Sir Cyril? He'd only met him the previous afternoon."

Lord Beaufort looked down at his notes. "That, my dear, is a question I would expect you to know the answer to. As I remember, you were present in the dining room when Mr Bell used threatening language towards Sir Cyril ... in fact, he made the threats after you'd traded words with the honourable gentleman."

Eliza's eyes were wide as she looked first at Lord Beaufort and then at Archie. "You can't seriously believe Father would murder someone just because of my silly argument."

"As I'm sure you'll appreciate, Mrs Thomson, we need to look at all possibilities and this is a scenario that fits the facts."

"Archie, tell him. Father wouldn't murder anyone."

Lord Beaufort held up his hand to silence Archie. "I'm afraid that as far as Mr Bell's concerned, Dr Thomson can't provide an unbiased opinion, and so I'd be grateful if you wouldn't put words into his mouth." He referred to his notes again. "Now, that's all we need from you, Mrs Thomson. Can you ask Soams to come in when you leave?"

"But what about my alibi and motive? Aren't you asking everyone the same questions?"

Lord Beaufort took off his spectacles and stared at her. "Oh my dear, we know you didn't do it. The strength needed to cause the injury rules out all the ladies. We only need to speak to you to check the alibis of the men. Now, run along and ask Soams to come in if you'd be so kind."

Eliza clenched her fists into her lap and glared at Lord Beaufort.

"Eliza, please." Archie's eyes held hers. "I need to leave by four but we still have more than half the guests to speak to."

With her face red, Eliza got to her feet and strode to the door, which she threw open before storming out, straight past Soams. *If I had a croquet mallet with me, I could make more than a dent in his head.*

Connie was waiting for her when she returned to the conservatory, but before she could relay any of the interview, Soams had joined them and summoned Connie to the library.

"How did you get on?" Mr Bell interrupted Eliza's thoughts as he joined her.

"It was terrible. They think you did it."

Mr Bell's face paled. "Me? Why would I do it?"

Eliza wiped the developing tears from her eyes. "I don't know, but Lord Beaufort was in the breakfast room when you threatened Sir Cyril, and the way he was talking, it sounded like he thinks that's a good enough motive. He suggested that the seconds you were alone together by the lake were enough for you to have killed him."

Mr Bell rubbed a hand across his face. "Where's he got that from? Who else was in the dining room when Sir Cyril was being rude to everyone?"

Eliza closed her eyes to think. "Connie and I, obviously, Henry, Caroline ... Lord Beaufort and Sir Cyril. That was it. Do you remember, when I arrived, Lord Beaufort was talking to Sir Cyril? He'll have heard the whole argument."

Mr Bell paced to the window. "What do I say? I can't

conjure up an alibi I don't have … but I didn't kill him. You know that, don't you?"

"Of course I do." Eliza's smile faded. "But I don't know what to say. At least Archie will be listening to the interviews; he should be able to talk some sense into him."

"I hope so, but he doesn't have the same flair for this sort of thing as you."

"Stop worrying, I'm sure everything will be fine once you get to tell your side of the story. It shouldn't be long now; people seem to be going in and out quite quickly. Here's Connie now."

Eliza's stomach churned when she saw the sullen look on Connie's face. She patted the seat beside her. "Come and sit down."

Connie glanced at Mr Bell but said nothing.

"I'll tell you what," Eliza said to Connie, "there's something I want to check up on. Why don't you and I go for a walk while the rest of the interviews are going on? There are still half a dozen people left, so we should have at least half an hour. You don't need us, do you, Father?"

"No, off you go. I can take care of myself. It's not as if you'd be able to come in with me."

"All right, well watch what you say and we'll see you later."

"Where are we going?" Connie asked as they walked past the bottom of the stairs and into the west wing. "We can't go outside without our coats."

"We're not going outside."

Connie's brow creased. "How can we go for a walk if we're not going outside?"

"We're going on a hunt for some shoes. I still have the

drawing in my handbag and I've been thinking that a good place to start would be the boot room. Lord Lowton's bound to have shoes in there ... and Lord Albert."

Connie's frown deepened. "How will we know who the shoes belong to?"

"We'll think about that when the time comes, now hurry up, I don't want anyone seeing us."

Eliza slowed down and peered into the rooms on both sides of the corridor as they approached the end of the west wing. "It must be around here somewhere. Ah ... steps. Come along."

"We can't go down there!" Connie said.

"We can if you hurry and don't make a noise." Eliza led the way down the stairs, which evidently led to the kitchen. The sound of the staff talking as they worked caused her to pause and study her surroundings. "In here." She grabbed Connie by the hand, pulling her through a small door to the right of the stairs, and closed it tightly behind them.

"Where are we?" Connie asked.

"I would say this is where they keep the shoes and boots for the whole family, wouldn't you? Some poor servant must have to keep this lot clean."

"I imagine they'll polish the shoes for the guests as well, looking at the number of shoes in here."

"Hmm, you could be right, let's hope so. Now, let's see what's here." Eliza took the sheet of paper from her bag and walked to a rack of men's shoes.

"Look here. These shoes have a monogram, C. L." Connie pointed to a pair of old brown walking boots.

Eliza picked up the shoes. "Let me have a look; C.L. Cyril Lowton. Yes, these shoes are bigger than the footprint, as were the shoes Sir Cyril wore on the day he died. Are there any with an N.L. marking?"

"Not here. How about A.L.? I presume that would be Albert Lowton, Lord Albert."

Eliza sat one of Lord Albert's right shoes over her sketch. "It could be. My drawing isn't as accurate as it should be but that could fit. The only problem is, don't you think Lord Albert is too slender to have made such a deep impression?"

Connie shrugged. "Dr Thomson said anyone could have made it if the ground was soft."

"He did. We'd better take one of these with us and check it for size against the real footprint."

"Now? Don't you think we need to get back?"

"Shhh, keep your voice down." Eliza froze as she listened for sounds outside. When she heard nothing, she put the shoe back in its place. "You're right, we'll need to come back. What else is there?"

"These are only small." Connie held up a pair of black leather ankle boots.

"So they are ... and they fit the sketch. Are there any markings on them?"

Connie turned both boots over in her hands and studied the insides. "No, nothing, but look, there are several rows with shoes of a similar size next to them."

"From the same person I'd say." Eliza examined each pair but found no trace of a monogram. "Don't you think it would be strange if Lord Lowton was the only member of the family who didn't have his shoes initialled?"

"Maybe the servants know which shoes are his and it's only those that don't belong to him that need monogramming."

"Perhaps, but in that case, I'm not sure how we prove these are his. Let me check the soles to see if there are any markings that match the footprint and then we'd better go."

By the time they arrived back in the hallway, the guests were filing into the drawing room for afternoon tea and a summary of the afternoon's findings.

"Just in time," Eliza said as she manoeuvred into the room ahead of Lords Lowton and Beaufort. "Father looks like he's saved us some seats."

With a cup of tea and a selection of sandwiches on a plate Eliza led Connie to their seats. "I wonder where Archie is."

"He came looking for you about ten minutes ago," Mr Bell said. "He said he needed to get back to Moreton and that he was already late so he'd see you later."

Eliza slumped into the chair. "How annoying, I wanted to find out what was said in the interviews."

"It looks like you're about to." Mr Bell nodded towards Lord Lowton, who stood in the middle of the room.

"Your attention, ladies and gentlemen. Lord Beaufort has an announcement."

"Ladies and gentlemen, thank you for indulging me this afternoon," Lord Beaufort started. "I appreciate many of you want to get home but I hope the magnificent hospitality of our hosts makes up for the delay." He took a sip of his tea.

"As you know, we were particularly interested in people's whereabouts for the hour between ten and eleven o'clock on Saturday morning. It's never easy to unravel the subtleties hidden within an interview, but in this case there was only one person with no alibi for the time of the murder." He paused as the door to the drawing room opened and Soams showed in two men in local police uniforms. "Mr George Bell, I've invited these police officers here today to arrest you for the murder of the Honourable Cyril Lowton."

"Me!" Mr Bell jumped to his feet, but the officers were upon him with a set of handcuffs. "I haven't done anything. All I did was find the body, you can't arrest me for that."

Eliza stood beside him. "He's right, you can't arrest him. You've got the wrong man."

"I'm afraid there's no mistake, madam. Mr Bell is the only man who could have done it." Lord Beaufort sat down and accepted a plate of sandwiches from a maid. "Thank you, Sergeant. You can take him away."

"Where are you taking him?" Eliza followed Mr Bell to the door. "Stop. I need to check with Archie. Are we sure he's actually left?" Eliza gestured to Connie to follow her. "He has to tell me what's been going on."

She stepped into the hallway in time to see Archie standing by the front door watching his father-in-law being led away.

"Archie, do something!" Eliza called.

"He won't help me." Mr Bell glowered at Archie, the venom in his voice obvious.

Archie glanced at Eliza before turning back to Mr Bell. "I didn't know he was going to have you arrested. I'm sorry, I did all I could."

"I bet you did..." Mr Bell's words faded as the door was closed behind him.

"Why didn't you do something?" Eliza said as she reached Archie's side.

"Because it's not that easy when you're dealing with people like this. Look, I'm sorry, I need to go. I'll see you later."

"Oh no you don't. You're already late so another half an hour won't make any difference. Father did not murder Sir Cyril and I need to know what happened in those interviews so we can make a case to get him released. He is not going to the gallows for another man's crime."

CHAPTER TWELVE

W ithout waiting for Archie to reply, Eliza stormed towards the stairs. "I'm going for my coat, I'll be down in one minute."

Good to her word, Eliza, with a panting Connie behind her, had no sooner disappeared than she returned to the hallway and headed towards the east wing.

"We can go out this way." She spoke to Archie without waiting for him.

"Eliza, calm down," Archie said once they were outside. "I'm sorry, I did everything I could, but it was like Lord Beaufort had already made his mind up about the outcome before he spoke to anyone."

Eliza stopped and planted her hands on her hips. "You mean there was a conspiracy to make sure he found Father guilty?"

"I wouldn't go so far as to say that, but Lord Beaufort accepted everyone's alibis without question, except your father's. I tried to intervene, but he closed me down. I had no say in the matter."

"He'll be sorry..." Eliza set off down the garden path again.

"Eliza, stop, please. These are powerful men we're dealing with. You can't just threaten them. Calm down and let's talk about it."

Eliza refused to look at Archie or Connie as tears welled in her eyes. "All right then, tell me what everyone said. What about Lord Lowton? Who provided him with an alibi?"

Archie hesitated. "He said he was in his office with Lord Beaufort, something that obviously wasn't questioned and they said no more of it."

"No more was said! I told you that when Father found Sir Cyril, at around half past ten, the first two people on the scene were Lord Lowton and his son, Albert. Didn't you ask how he miraculously got from the office to the lake in less than a minute?"

"No..."

"Was mention even made of the fact that Lord Lowton was there when Father found the body ... and there was no sign of Lord Beaufort?"

Eliza wiped her eyes as she glared at Archie.

"No, I'm sorry, I'd forgotten he was on the scene ... but he's a commanding figure and he spoke with such authority. He said that he was in his office with Lord Beaufort and when Beaufort agreed I could hardly say I didn't believe them."

"And so what about Lord Forsyth, who provided his alibi?"

"He didn't really have one. He said he was in the snooker room waiting for Henry and Lords David and Albert."

"And did anyone confirm that?"

Archie shook his head. "No, but when I questioned it, Lord Beaufort implied that because he's an earl, his testimony's above reproach."

"So he didn't have an alibi, but because of his title, his statement was taken at face value?"

"When we were going through the evidence at the end of the session, I tried again to question Lord Beaufort's faith in the alibis, but he told me not to interfere."

"And did the boys confirm they were heading for the snooker room? I find it hard to believe Lord Albert planned to be there given he was by the lake."

"Lord Albert said he'd arranged to meet his uncle, but had gone for his usual walk around the lake where he was delayed by your father."

"So where were Henry and Lord David?"

Archie sighed. "That was rather awkward. Henry looked very sheepish when Lord Beaufort questioned him but finally admitted he'd been walking in the gardens with Lady Alice."

"He was with Lady Alice ... after we told him to stay away from her?" Eliza was no longer sure who to be more furious with. "Did she confirm his statement?"

"No. She was most indignant about it all, even saying that Lord Beaufort was quite mad if he believed she would hit her uncle around the head with a croquet mallet."

"But she confirmed she was with Henry?"

"No, she refused to say where she was. She said that as she had done nothing wrong, it was none of our business."

"It sounds like the sort of thing someone would say if they had something to hide," Connie said.

Archie smiled at her. "You're right, but I got the

impression she was more bothered about admitting to being with Henry than anything else."

Eliza put her hands to her head. "We have to get Henry away from here before he gets himself into trouble. I need to stay here so I can visit Father in the morning, but could you take him? I want him out of the way."

Archie shrugged. "I suppose so."

"It might be a good time for you to talk to him, as well. He wanted to see you anyway, so this would be a good excuse for you to spend time with him."

"Has he told you what he wants?"

"No, he wouldn't say. To be honest, he's been quite cold with me over the weekend but I don't know why. I was hoping to talk to him on the journey, but it will have to wait now."

Archie put an arm around Eliza's shoulders as they continued towards the lake. "I'll speak to him."

Eliza nodded, and they continued to walk in silence until Connie broke the tension.

"Dr Thomson, you didn't tell us what Lord David was doing at the time of the murder. Was he with Henry and Lady Alice?"

"Ah, no, he actually said he'd been in his room, reading."

Eliza raised an eyebrow. "And so he had no one to confirm his alibi either? Lord Beaufort specifically said Father was the only one without an alibi, but that's patently a lie. Any one of them could have done it ... even him. You don't think he's involved, do you, and putting the blame on Father?"

Archie closed his eyes and took a deep breath. "I doubt

that one of the most senior judges in the country would cover up a murder."

"You have too much faith in human nature. I don't like the sound of this at all. It's as if they're trying to protect themselves."

"What about Sir Rodney?" Connie asked. "He's not one of them, what did he say?"

"Yes, that was interesting," Archie said. "He'd gone for a walk in the grounds and had seen Mr Bell walking with you. He said he increased his pace to catch you up but as he did, your father turned towards the lake and so he slowed down again."

"He must have been nearby when Father shouted then," Eliza said. "Everyone within a hundred feet must have heard him."

"I managed to ask him that, but he said he heard nothing. He ended up walking down the left-hand side of the lake and so he could have been out of the way by the time your father shouted."

"So technically he had no alibi either?" Eliza stared at Archie. "What is going on here?"

"Do you think they're all lying?" Connie asked.

"I'd be amazed if they weren't, but I'm afraid they've picked the wrong man to put the blame on. If they think I'm going to rest while the real killer walks free, they can think again."

"What will you do?" Connie asked. "They won't like you asking any more questions."

"No, they won't." Eliza paused and studied her husband. "We need to get the police involved."

"The police are already involved."

"The local police don't count. We need to contact the police in London."

Archie's face paled. "Eliza, you can't do that, you heard what Lord Lowton said."

"I don't care what Lord Lowton said. That was before he got Father arrested. The local police will only ever do what he tells them and so we need to go above them. As soon as you get home, I'd like you to send a telegram to Inspector Adams at New Scotland Yard. He's the only person I can turn to and after Mrs Milwood's death last year, hopefully he'll trust me enough to take me seriously. Can you ask him to come to Lowton police station as early as possible tomorrow morning? I'll visit Father in the morning and make sure they don't move him anywhere until the inspector arrives."

Connie clapped her hands beneath her chin. "What a splendid idea. Inspector Adams thought you did a marvellous job last year."

Eliza smiled. "He was glad of our help and so I'm hoping he'll return the favour. Will you promise me you'll contact him?"

Archie rubbed a hand across his face. "You can't expect him to drop everything to come straight over."

Eliza rummaged in her handbag until she found a blank sheet of paper. "I need him to come quickly. I haven't asked Caroline about staying yet and although I'm sure she'll say yes, we can't stay here indefinitely. Let me write something."

Please come to Lowton Pol. Stn urgently. Serious miscarriage of justice. Need help. Eliza Thomson.

She handed the paper to Archie. "What do you think?"

"I suppose it should do the trick." Archie sighed. "Leave

it with me and while I'm at it, I'll call the coroner. I don't want your father to hang any more than you do."

Eliza threw her arms around Archie's neck. "Thank you, I'm so frightened for him. Did you see the look on his face when they led him away? He was so confused."

"I saw the anger on his face." Archie grimaced.

"Well, we need to work out how we can get him out of this." Eliza took Archie's arm as they turned to walk back to the house.

"We must find Henry as well if he's going back to Moreton with you. Let me ask Soams for some tea while we search for him."

Archie checked his pocket watch. "I haven't got time for tea. I should have gone over an hour ago. Let's just find Henry and then we can go."

"He could be anywhere," Connie said. "We've not seen much of him this weekend."

"He may be in the library if he has studying to do," Archie said.

Eliza rolled her eyes. "Don't be ridiculous. Our best hope is that he's in the snooker room with Lord Albert. If he's with Lady Alice, goodness knows where he'll be, and I doubt he'll surface until he gets hungry."

"What about checking his room?" Archie said.

"I most certainly hope they're not up there together." Eliza gaped at her husband.

"No, I didn't mean together, I meant by himself. You know he likes his sleep..."

"Not that much, he doesn't." Eliza led them into the west wing. "The snooker room is at the end of this corridor."

Once they arrived, Eliza stopped outside the door and

turned to Archie. "You knock and put your head around the door. Rooms like this aren't intended for women."

Archie did as he was asked but backed out of the room almost immediately.

"He's not there?" Eliza's heart sank.

"The room's empty. What do we do now?"

They paused as Soams appeared from the steps leading down to the kitchen. "May I help you, sir?"

"We're looking for our son Henry. I don't suppose you've seen him?"

Soams paused. "I last saw him heading down the garden with Lord Albert and Lady Alice. They looked to be heading towards the croquet lawn. You can see that part of the garden from the window in the library if you care to check."

Eliza's heart fluttered; she wasn't sure whether to be relieved or fearful. "Thank you, we will." She set off at a brisk pace as Connie and Archie hurried after her. "We must get him away from Lady Alice. I only hope Lord Albert's still with them."

Minutes later, Eliza pushed open the library door and hurried to the window. "They're not there." Her heart raced as she strained to see beyond the corner of the house. "What's he thinking of? I haven't told him I'm not going home and so he should be ready and waiting to travel with me."

"Shall we take a walk and see if they're close by?" Connie asked.

Archie walked back to the door. "I'm sorry, but I must go. He'll have to come home with you if he still wants to talk to me."

"Well, it's to be hoped I'm not here for long. He's due back in Cambridge next weekend."

Eliza and Connie followed Archie into the hallway and waited while Soams arranged for someone to bring the carriage around to the front.

"Don't get so upset with him," Archie said. "He's a young boy, enjoying himself. I'm sure I was the same at his age."

"I'm sure you weren't!" Eliza's angst faded under Archie's gaze, her lips turning into a grin. "At least not around titled ladies."

Archie returned her grin. "Write to me tomorrow and tell me what you're doing ... and keep me up to date with how your father is. I'll do what I can to help."

He leaned forward and kissed Eliza on the forehead before smiling at Connie. "You will keep an eye on her, won't you? Don't let her think she's a detective."

"She's a very good detective," Connie said, before Archie gave her a lopsided grin and headed towards the front door.

"Shouldn't we have asked Lady Caroline about staying before Archie left?" Connie asked as the carriage disappeared around the bend in the drive.

The glint returned to Eliza's eye. "Then she would have had an excuse to say no. This way, we can't get home until tomorrow, even if we wanted to. Come along, let's go and see if we can find her."

As soon as they entered the front door, Soams showed them into the drawing room where Lady Caroline stood by the window at the far end of the room.

"Eliza, darling," she said as they walked in. "How

dreadful for you to find out about your father. I'm still in shock myself. Imagine one's godfather being a murderer."

Eliza and Connie took seats opposite their hostess. "He's not a murderer, Caroline, no more than you or I. Someone wants him to take the blame for their crime."

"I'm sure that's how it must look, but Lord Beaufort isn't a law lord for no reason."

"I need to speak to Father tomorrow ... at the police station. Do you mind if we stay here another night?"

"Here? Well, I don't know, I'm not sure what Neville will say."

"Please, Caroline. We've been friends for years and it should only be for another night or two. I'm sure Father had nothing to do with the death of Sir Cyril; I just need to prove it."

Lady Caroline's eyes bored into Eliza before she nodded. "Very well. He is my godfather and I suppose we should abide by the notion that he's innocent until proven guilty. Leave Neville to me. I'll explain."

Eliza released the breath she had been holding. "Thank you. We'll try to stay out of Lord Lowton's way."

"I think that would be for the best, although you'll probably see him at dinner. I'll explain that you expect them to take Mr Bell to London at the first opportunity and that when they do, you'll go with him."

Eliza nodded. "I suppose they will. We'll have to wait and see. I just hope they'll let me speak to him first."

"Of course you do." Lady Caroline rang a bell she kept on the side table and waited for Soams to respond. "Could you pour us all a brandy, Soams? Mrs Thomson and her friend are in shock ... and I can't let them drink alone."

Soams bowed and backed out of the room, just as Lord Lowton came in.

"Darling, have you seen...?" He stopped when he saw Eliza and Connie. "Oh, you're still here?"

"Yes, they're in shock and need to visit Mr Bell at the police station tomorrow," Lady Caroline said. "I've said they can stay until he's moved to London. It should only be for a day or two."

Eliza noticed the twitch return to Lord Lowton's left eye.

"Yes, of course..."

"Are Archie and Henry still here?" Lady Caroline asked.

"Archie had to get back to Moreton, but Henry is still here ... somewhere. Soams said he was last seen with Lord Albert."

Lord Lowton glared at Eliza, but was distracted by his wife.

"That's nice. Now, Neville, what were you going to tell me you've lost?"

"Lost? Nothing..."

Lady Caroline rolled her eyes at Eliza. "You came in here asking if I'd seen something. That means you've lost the said something."

"Yes, of course. One of my cufflinks ... the gold ones I was wearing on Saturday morning."

"Did it have...?" Connie stopped abruptly as Eliza kicked the side of her ankle.

"What was that?" Lord Lowton turned to face her.

"Nothing ... I-I just wondered ... if you still had the other one. If we could see it, we might be able to help you find it."

"Or maybe you didn't put them in their usual place," Eliza added.

"My man usually takes them from the cuffs and puts them away for me, but he doesn't remember seeing them on Saturday. He was too busy getting me ready for the ball, I suppose, but he's just gone to lift them out for the morning and there's only one."

"It must have fallen onto the floor," Lady Caroline said. "Have you asked the maids?"

Lord Lowton studied the three women before heading for the door. "No, not yet ... I'll get Soams to check."

CHAPTER THIRTEEN

Eliza stood at the bedroom window, staring out over the garden as the sun rose. It wasn't yet half past six, and although she was never usually awake at this hour, she knew she wouldn't get any more sleep. That had evaded her all night. How was she going to make a case to get her father released? It would be her word against Lord Beaufort's and she wouldn't stand a chance. There had to be something she could do.

The clock had just struck seven when there was a knock on the bedroom door and she answered it to find Connie standing in her nightdress.

"Oh good, you're awake. A maid's brought us a pot of tea."

Eliza walked into the sitting room and flopped onto the settee. "I feel as if I've been awake all night trying to work out how to clear Father's name. I keep running over the events in my mind but I can't see a way out." Eliza banged a hand on the arm of the chair. "Damn Caroline and her stupid party."

Connie handed Eliza a cup and saucer and sat on the

chair opposite. "Here, take this. We do have some evidence we could use against Lord Lowton."

"We do, but it's not very strong and it'll only work if he was the killer. I mean, why would he murder his own brother?"

"You don't think the argument between Sir Cyril and Lady Caroline would be enough?"

Eliza shook her head. "That would be like saying Father would murder Archie because he doesn't like him. It's not plausible."

"It might not be, but I'm sure you could make a case against him if you tried."

Eliza took a sip of the over-sweetened tea and screwed up her face. "Maybe. Last night, after you'd gone to bed, I wrote out everything we know so far so we can take it to Father. The problem is, seeing it all written out like that makes the evidence look rather flimsy. Not to mention the fact that Lord Lowton has Lord Beaufort on his side. I'm sure they'd discredit anything we throw at them."

"Come on, it's not like you to be so down. Inspector Adams should arrive today and we can take him through all the evidence. He may be able to help."

Eliza nodded. "I'm sorry, I just feel so helpless and getting no sleep has only made it worse. You're right about Inspector Adams though."

"That's more like it." Connie smiled as she stood up. "Now, I suggest we both get dressed and go down for breakfast before we leave the house. You need something to eat if you want a clear head."

. . .

An hour later, they walked down the stairs to the breakfast room.

"Thank goodness Lord Lowton isn't here," Eliza said.

"He's been and gone, madam." Eliza jumped as Soams crept up behind her. "Lady Caroline usually arrives at about half past eight. The breakfasts are not so lavish when we're not entertaining. May I get you some toast and marmalade?"

"Yes, please, that would be lovely." Eliza glanced at the clock and waited for Soams to disappear. "We've got about twenty minutes before Caroline arrives, time to go through the evidence I wrote out last night. I'd rather not share any of it with her at the moment."

"Don't you think she could help?"

Eliza shook her head. "She was too busy organising everything for the ball on Saturday; she won't have seen anything, and I'd rather not tell her what we're doing in case she mentions anything to Lord Lowton. I don't want him finding out."

Eliza spread her papers on the table but immediately collected them up again as Soams returned. She waited for him to leave before straightening them out again. "Don't these people have any respect for privacy? Now, let's see what we've got."

They talked through the details of the murder scene and wondered about taking the shoe to the lake to confirm who had made the footprint. They were only starting on the alibis when Lady Caroline joined them.

"You're down early." Lady Caroline swept into the room in an elaborate dressing gown. "I thought you'd have had a lie-in."

"No." Eliza took a deep breath before she continued. "I

didn't sleep well worrying about Father. He must have had a dreadful night."

"Oh my, I'd quite forgotten."

Forgotten! How on earth...? Eliza stared at her friend.

"I don't think Eliza's likely to forget," Connie said. "It's a difficult time."

"Of course, I quite understand." Lady Caroline helped herself to a cup of tea.

Eliza glanced at Connie and nodded towards the door. "I'm sorry we can't stay but we really need to get to the police station. Will you excuse us?"

Eliza didn't wait for a reply before she pushed the papers into her bag and stood up, walking out without a backward glance.

"Living the life of lady of the manor's changed her more than I thought," Eliza said as she and Connie climbed into a carriage. "She would never have forgotten something like that before she had any of this. It's as well we said nothing to her."

The journey to the police station only took five minutes and Mr Bell looked up with red eyes as the desk sergeant showed them through the reception and down a corridor to his cell.

"Eliza, Constance. You came." He dashed to the bars of the cell.

"Of course we came, what did you expect? We're going to get you out of here."

The sergeant was about to unlock the cell door when he stopped and frowned at Eliza.

"No, I don't mean we're going to break him out." Eliza took a deep breath. "We'll do it legally and with permission."

"Sorry, madam, I misunderstood." The sergeant opened the cell door to let them in.

"Thank you, Sergeant. Would you be so kind as to give us some privacy? We have details of the case we'd like to discuss and I'm expecting Inspector Adams from New Scotland Yard to join us shortly. Can you tell me if you get a telegram from him?"

"Lord Lowton's called in New Scotland Yard?" The sergeant stared at Eliza. "He said he wanted to keep it between ourselves."

"Lord Lowton might want to keep it quiet, but he's had my father arrested and I'm not happy about it. I've called in New Scotland Yard."

"You?" A smirk crossed the sergeant's face. "Well, yes, I'll be sure to tell you if a telegram arrives."

Mr Bell gestured for them to sit on the edge of the stone slab that passed as a bed. "I'm sorry I can't offer you a chair."

Eliza glanced around the cramped cell with damp stone walls and a tiny square of a window well above head height. "They wouldn't keep animals in a place like this. We must get you out."

"I won't argue with that. The food could be better as well."

Eliza's shoulders slumped. "What was I thinking? I should have brought something for you. I will next time we come."

"I hope there won't be a next time. I'd like to get out of here. Have you really called in the Yard?"

Eliza smiled. "I have, I had to do something. Lord Beaufort won't help us and the police around here will only do what Lord Lowton tells them."

"Do you know this Inspector Adams?"

"I do. When we were investigating the murder in the village last year, he was assigned to the case. We got off to an unfortunate start, but once he knew I was your daughter, he changed his mind." Eliza's brow furrowed. "Come to think of it, he never did say how he knew you. Anyway, he's the only inspector in London I know and so I thought I'd ask him to help. It can't do any harm, can it? Archie promised to send him a telegram when he got back to Moreton."

"Archie! Well, you can forget any idea of the inspector calling then. That husband of yours was as much responsible for having me arrested as Lord Beaufort."

"That's not true. I spoke to him after you'd left and he did his best, but it's not easy. You said yourself, Lord Lowton and Lord Beaufort are both powerful men and Lord Beaufort had no interest in listening to him. He's sorry for what's happened and wants to help."

"Fiddlesticks he does, he's just saying that."

"Father, stop, this isn't helping anything. We need to go through the evidence and see if there's anything else you can help us with. Once the inspector arrives, I'm hoping he'll let Connie and I accompany him while he interviews everyone properly. From what Archie said, Lord Beaufort made a terrible job of it. Half the men there didn't have an alibi and yet he still picked on you."

"We think it's because you were the only one without a title," Connie said.

Mr Bell's face twisted as he studied Connie. "But that's preposterous!"

"We know, but Dr Thomson said Lord Beaufort was more inclined to believe the alibis of the titled men."

"Is this true?" Mr Bell turned to Eliza. "Why didn't he challenge him?"

"He did, but Lord Beaufort wouldn't listen. Now, enough of him. Let's go through what we've found out so far." Eliza took a bunch of papers from her handbag. "We'll start on Saturday morning. When we were walking down the left-hand side of the garden, you saw Sir Cyril walking across the lower path towards the rhododendron bushes."

Mr Bell nodded.

"Now, you told me, and we saw, that by the time you reached the bushes, Sir Cyril had disappeared behind them."

"He had, but when I reached the side of the bushes, I wasn't sure which way he'd gone. That's when I paused to get my bearings. I'd just decided which way to go when I heard a loud cracking sound..."

"Which we now believe was the sound of the croquet mallet on Sir Cyril's head."

"Correct."

Eliza added a few notes to her paper. "Before we go on, do you remember seeing Sir Cyril with a croquet mallet when he was on the path?"

Mr Bell shook his head. "I can't say I did ... although I couldn't rule it out. I was focussing on his face to see if there was an ounce of remorse on it, which there wasn't. He seemed distracted ... I'm not even sure he saw me."

"It sounds like he might have been up to something," Eliza said.

"But why would he be carrying a croquet mallet?" Connie asked. "If that was the murder weapon, it would be the murderer who took it to the scene, not the victim."

Eliza nodded. "You're right, it was just a thought.

Besides, we know the mallet went missing after we had hidden it in the bushes and Sir Cyril couldn't have moved it."

"Which suggests someone knows more about this than they're telling us," Connie said.

Eliza made another note on her paper. "It does, but we need to find that mallet. It must be around somewhere."

"How do we do that?" Connie stared at Eliza. "The house is huge, not to mention the size of the gardens. It could be anywhere."

"It could be, but we need to be clever about this and think of a logical place to put it. It can't have gone far." After a second's pause, she turned back to Mr Bell. "What happened after you heard the croquet mallet on Sir Cyril's head?"

"Well, there was the splash. At the time I had no idea what it was."

"And that's when you hurried to the other side of the bushes?"

"Precisely."

"So, let's stop there. We need to go back and check how long it would have taken you to hurry from the fork in the path to the scene of the crime. The bushes are big, but I imagine it took no more than ten seconds or so, which means the killer must have moved quickly to escape the scene. You're sure you didn't see or hear anything ... someone hiding in the bushes, perhaps."

"No, by the time I'd rounded the corner the path was empty. I didn't even notice Sir Cyril until he floated to the surface of the water."

Eliza nodded. "All right, so that confirms what we've thought all along. Someone must have been with Sir Cyril as

113

you stood on the footpath not twenty feet away. Unfortunately, by the time you reached the scene, the culprit had disappeared."

"It must have been someone quick on their feet," Connie said.

"Either that, or they didn't go very far and were close enough to watch what happened next." Eliza turned to her father. "What did happen next?"

"Well, as I've told you, I panicked and called for help. It's not every day you find a dead body ... not that I knew he was dead at the time. That's why I jumped into the lake to try and save him."

Eliza stopped her writing and looked up. "You jumped in? You didn't mention that before."

Mr Bell shrugged. "I thought it was obvious. The water isn't deep, less than waist height, and so I decided it was the best way to get Sir Cyril out."

Eliza sucked the end of her pencil. "Yes, I'd forgotten that ... and so you were standing in the water, trying to haul the body onto the path when Lord Lowton arrived?"

Mr Bell nodded. "Lord Albert got there first, but Lord Lowton wasn't far behind."

"And we came as soon as we heard you shout. How many times did you call out?"

Mr Bell blew out through his mouth. "I'm not sure, a couple of times, maybe three."

"I only heard you once, and that was as we approached the bushes," Eliza said. "Assuming you left a couple of seconds between each call, and assuming Lords Lowton and Albert heard the first call, they must have been on the scene within ten to fifteen seconds of you shouting. Don't you think that's strange?"

"I suppose it is now you mention it," Mr Bell said. "The thing I thought most strange at the time, though, is that they came from opposite directions."

"Yes, I remember that. Did they seem surprised to see each other?"

"Surprised. Why would they?" Connie asked.

"Because as you said yourself, the house and the grounds are huge and yet they were both within feet of the murder scene but not together. Not only that, Lord Lowton himself said that people rarely visit that spot and that the body could have been there for days had Father not found it."

"And yet they were both close at hand." Connie's forehead creased. "Dr Thomson said that Lord Albert was taking a walk around the lake, which was something he was fond of doing..."

"And which would have taken him to that spot on a regular basis," Mr Bell said.

"It would." Eliza stood up and paced the cell. "But we don't know why Lord Lowton was there. When Lord Beaufort interviewed him, Archie said they confirmed each other's alibis that they were both in his office, but neither of them mentioned that at around half past ten, Lord Lowton was by the lake."

"Why would he have been there if it was a place he rarely visited?"

Eliza shook her head. "That's a good question. He's got to know more than he's telling us. We just need to find out what it is."

CHAPTER FOURTEEN

Eliza stood up and paced the cell for the umpteenth time.

"What on earth's keeping him? It's nearly noon already."

Connie's shoulders sagged as she played with her fingers. "You don't know for certain he'll come. He may be busy with something else."

"Connie's right," Mr Bell said. "I don't suppose he can just drop everything and come rushing over here for me."

Eliza perched once more on the edge of the bed. "You're right but I had hoped he would. He was grateful last year for everything we did and I suppose I thought that would be enough."

Mr Bell patted his daughter's hand. "Don't be so down. Once I get to London, I'll call my solicitor and see if they can sort something out. You've done everything you can."

"But it's not enough, is it? You shouldn't even be in here..." Eliza paused as the outside door opened and the police sergeant walked into the room with a piece of paper in his hand. Eliza jumped to her feet. "Is that a telegram for me?"

The sergeant gave his familiar patronising smile. "It is a telegram, but not for you. We've been told to move the prisoner to Bow Street in London. We can't keep violent criminals here."

"He is not a violent criminal, look at him. He's been wrongly accused." Eliza took a deep breath and calmed her voice again before continuing. "Please, can you give us a little more time? I'm sure Inspector Adams will be here shortly."

"Sorry, madam. The constable's getting the carriage ready to move him and so I'd suggest you say your farewells. You'll need to apply for permission to visit once he's in London." The sergeant turned on his heel, the smirk still on his face.

"Stop worrying." Mr Bell took Eliza's hand. "As soon as my solicitor hears what's happened, he'll get me out. Why don't you come to Richmond on Saturday and I'll see you there?"

"All right, just promise you'll write to me as soon as you're free. I won't let this rest until they catch the real murderer."

Mr Bell nodded as the sergeant returned and fastened his hands and feet in chains. "As long as you promise me you'll be careful."

"Of course I will." Eliza wiped a tear from her eye before picking up her bag to follow them outside. They stepped onto the footpath and she shuddered as the door to the carriage slammed shut. "This shouldn't be happening," she said to Connie. "How could anyone think he's a murderer?"

The driver clambered up to his seat and was about to

leave when a second carriage pulled up behind them and a man of medium build with dark hair and a pencil-thin moustache got out.

Eliza did a double take as she realised what was happening and leapt forward to wave her arms at her father's driver. "Stop, please! Just wait one more minute."

"Good morning, Mrs Thomson, Mrs Appleton." Inspector Adams extended a hand to each of them. "It seems I've arrived just in time."

The smile dropped from the sergeant's face as the inspector beckoned the driver.

"Do as the lady says and bring the prisoner back inside. I'd like to hear what's been going on before he's moved."

Eliza breathed a sigh of relief as she and Connie followed the inspector back into the station and into the sergeant's office.

"Good afternoon, Inspector ... and thank you for coming. I assure you I wouldn't have asked you all the way over here if it wasn't important."

The inspector ushered them into the office and closed the door behind them. "I hope you're right. Do you want to tell me what's been going on?"

It took Eliza less than five minutes to give the inspector the relevant details of the house party, the death of Sir Cyril and the arrest of Mr Bell.

"So it's your father you believe has been wrongfully arrested?"

Eliza nodded. "He had an alibi for all but about half a minute of the time leading up to the death. He couldn't have killed anyone in that time ... but even if he had, he wouldn't have called for help as quickly as he did. Whoever murdered

Sir Cyril probably hoped that the body wouldn't be found for days."

"So why was your father arrested?"

"Lord Lowton didn't want the death investigated because he said it would bring scandal to the village, but when I insisted, his good friend Lord Beaufort, the law lord, took charge of the investigation. He interviewed all the guests on Sunday afternoon, but if I'm allowed to be frank, he did an appalling job. All he did was make a note of the guests' alibis, he didn't even consider their motives."

Inspector Adams frowned. "How do you know this? Did you sit in on the interviews?"

"No, I wish I had, but it was out of the question. Fortunately, when I suspected foul play, I asked my husband, Dr Thomson, to come to Lowton to complete the death certificate. His Lordship wasn't very pleased, but I persuaded him he'd be discreet. I also arranged for Dr Thomson to sit in on the interviews so he could ask any questions relevant to the murder."

"I'm assuming from what you've said that he didn't do that."

"No, he wasn't given the chance. Lord Beaufort cut him off whenever he had a question and refused to discuss the evidence at the end of the afternoon. Lord Beaufort believes anyone with a title is above reproach but the problem is, none of them had a firm alibi."

"And so you want me to overrule a law lord and start a new investigation?"

Eliza's cheeks coloured as the inspector stared at her. "Please, would you? Someone must be lying, but we can't interview them on our own."

Inspector Adams stood up and walked to the door. "What makes you think I can? We're not dealing with the low life of London here."

"No, but you have more authority than we do."

Inspector Adams sighed. "I can't promise anything, but let me hear what Mr Bell has to say. If we believe a member of the aristocracy has committed the crime, I'll have to involve the chief constable ... and we'll need watertight evidence."

Eliza nodded. "We do have some evidence that might be significant."

"Mrs Thomson suspects Lord Lowton might be involved," Connie said.

Inspector Adams' shoulders visibly sank. "Lord Lowton?" He shook his head as he opened the door. "This had better be good."

A moment later, the constable opened the door to the cell and Eliza introduced Inspector Adams to her father.

"Good grief, Mr Bell, how good to see you again." Inspector Adams offered him his hand.

"*Inspector* Adams? My, you've done well for yourself."

"So you do know each other." Eliza smiled for the first time that day.

Mr Bell nodded. "I didn't recognise the name earlier because the inspector here was a mere constable when we last met."

"And it's thanks to you I got my promotion when I did." The inspector turned to talk to Eliza. "About eight years ago, your father's workshop fell victim to a spate of burglaries. Once we'd completed the investigation and had the gang locked up, he wrote to the chief constable to put in a good word for me. I was made up to sergeant almost immediately and inspector two years after that."

"Well, I'm glad I could help. I always like to recognise men who work hard. I just hope you can help me out of the mess I've found myself in."

"Mrs Thomson's given me some background into the death. Do you want to tell me where you were at the time?"

Mr Bell relayed the same information he had discussed earlier with Eliza.

"All right." The inspector lowered his voice. "Tell me about Lord Lowton. Why do you think he might be involved?"

Eliza once again took her papers from her bag. "First of all, I think he was angry with Sir Cyril."

"You think? We're going to have to do better than that."

"Well, actually, it was Lady Caroline who was furious with Sir Cyril and she wanted Lord Lowton to make sure he didn't attend the ball that evening."

"Murdering someone is quite a drastic way to stop them going to a ball!"

Eliza's face coloured. "I know, but there were tensions between them on the Friday evening that stem from when Lady Caroline married into the family. She wasn't a lady at the time, you see, and Sir Cyril wasn't happy about it."

"How long ago was that?"

"About twenty years," Connie said.

"So why suddenly murder him now if the rivalry's been going on for so long?" Inspector Adams asked. "I'm sorry, but we'll need more than that."

"Well, we found a footprint at the scene of the crime that could belong to Lord Lowton. It's on the edge of the water and it's too small for Sir Cyril's feet." Eliza handed the drawing of the footprint to the inspector.

"But you've already said that Lord Lowton was close by when the body was found, and it is his estate. Finding a footprint that might be his is hardly a surprise. Besides, didn't you say his son was also at the scene? It could be his footprint."

"It could but we need to check. We've found the boot room in the house and want to find the shoes that made the mark."

Inspector Adams grimaced. "Even if the print is Lord Lowton's it won't prove he murdered his brother."

Eliza flicked through her notes as she struggled to hide the tears that were forming.

"I suppose the same would be true of the fact we found one of Lord Lowton's cufflinks at the scene as well," Connie said. "He admits he lost it on Saturday."

"I'm sorry, all this might be helpful if Lord Lowton didn't own the estate. As it is, we'll have to come up with more than that."

"There is one thing that's strange," Mr Bell said. "Lord Lowton was on the scene of the crime too quickly. No sooner had I called for help than he and Lord Albert were with me."

Inspector Adams shrugged. "Again, it doesn't make either of them murderers. They may have had perfectly legitimate reasons for being there."

"But if they did, why didn't they mention them to Lord Beaufort?"

Inspector Adams narrowed his eyes. "Go on."

"When they gave their alibis, Lord Lowton said he had been in his office with Lord Beaufort, something the latter agreed with. Neither mentioned the fact that Lord Lowton had left to go into the gardens ... or that he was with me seconds after I found the body."

Inspector Adams studied his notebook. "You said the murder took place at about half past ten."

"Exactly. The alibis were meant to cover the time between ten and eleven that morning, but there were at least four people who knew Lord Lowton was by the lake when we found the body. He clearly wasn't in his office for the full hour, so why would he lie?"

"All right, that's something to work on. What about Lord Albert? Was he with his father?"

"No, he came from the opposite direction," Mr Bell said.

"But he has no one to support his alibi," Eliza added. "He said he'd been walking around the lake when he heard Father shout. The thing is, when Lord Lowton was trying to conceal the death he said very few people ever went to that spot and had it not been for Father, the body could have been in the water for days."

"But that can't be true, because Lord Albert said he often walks around the lake," Connie added.

"All right," Inspector Adams said. "Let's assume for a moment there is enough to question them, why would Lord Lowton kill his brother, or Lord Albert his uncle?"

"Perhaps Lord Lowton had had enough of Sir Cyril constantly criticising his wife?" Connie said. Inspector Adams shook his head. "We'd never be able to prosecute him on that. It's too weak. What about Lord Albert?"

Eliza shook her head. "I would say he was more like his uncle than his father, but we didn't really see much of him."

"Do you think Henry might be able to help?" Mr Bell

said. "He's studying with him at Cambridge and has spent a lot of time with him these last few weeks."

"That's an idea." Eliza turned to Connie. "We need to speak to him when we go back to the house later."

"You're still staying there?" Inspector Adams raised an eyebrow.

"While Father's in here, Lady Caroline has said we can stay at the hall for as long as we want. That's why I'd rather he wasn't moved to London. It gives us an excuse to stay there."

Inspector Adams wrote in his notebook. "What about the other guests? You said yourself, most had alibis that weren't confirmed. Do you know if any of them had a motive?"

Eliza shrugged. "We haven't really focussed on anyone else to be honest. The only other men who were there were Sir Cyril's son, Lord David; Lord Forsyth, who's married to Sir Cyril's sister; Lord Beaufort and Sir Rodney, Lady Caroline's father."

Once he'd finished writing, Inspector Adams turned to Connie. "You suggested Lord Lowton may have murdered his brother because he criticised his wife, but what if it was Lady Caroline's father who was protecting her? What was his alibi?"

"Rodney? He wouldn't do such a thing," Mr Bell said. "And he certainly wouldn't let me hang for it."

"You never can tell what goes on inside the mind of a murderer," the inspector said. "Has he ever mentioned the way Sir Cyril treated his daughter?

"Not directly," Eliza said, "but I did sit next to him for dinner on Friday evening and he mentioned how he and his wife, Lady Rosemary, didn't always see eye to eye with Sir Cyril."

"His alibi can't be confirmed either," Connie added.

The inspector raised an eyebrow. "Where was he?"

"He told Lord Beaufort he had been walking around the grounds alone."

"And Lord Beaufort didn't question him further?" Inspector Adams' eyebrows were so low they almost concealed his eyes.

"No. According to Dr Thomson the only person he questioned in any detail was Father."

Inspector flicked back through his notebook. "You said your son Henry was there. Was his alibi robust?"

"Henry! What motive would he have for murdering a man he'd never met before?"

"You need to be honest, Eliza," Mr Bell said.

Eliza glanced from her father to the inspector, who was staring at her. "All right, Henry and Sir Cyril had had a few words on Friday evening, that's all."

"What about?"

Eliza sighed. "Over the weekend, Henry's been taken with Lord Lowton's daughter, Lady Alice. On the Friday evening Sir Cyril caught them sitting a little too closely to each other. He caused rather a scene about it before demanding that Henry stay away from her."

"And so Henry could have wanted his revenge?"

"No, not at all. He doesn't worry about things like that and I told him that Lord Lowton wanted him and his friends in the dining room. They left before Sir Cyril had finished his tantrum."

"What was his alibi for the time of the murder?"

Eliza shook her head. "He said he was with Lady Alice, but she refused to confirm it, probably for obvious reasons."

"Or possibly because it wasn't true?" Inspector Adams paused to study Eliza.

"No, I'm sure it was. Dr Thomson told us that when Lady Alice was questioned, she was quite indignant about it all given that there was no possibility she could have killed her uncle."

"And Lord Beaufort accepted that?"

"He seemed to."

Inspector Adams leaned back in his chair and studied Eliza. "Suppose Henry and Lady Alice had been together in the grounds and Sir Cyril had seen them again? It could be that words were exchanged and a fight broke out which led to Sir Cyril's death."

Eliza closed her eyes to restrain the tears she could sense forming. "No, he wouldn't..."

Mr Bell was on his feet. "No! We brought you here to help us not accuse an innocent boy of murder."

Inspector Adams held up his hands. "I'm not saying he did it but we need to work through all the possibilities because if we don't, someone else will."

"This is ludicrous..." Mr Bell retook his seat.

Inspector Adams turned to Eliza. "Did you say Henry was still at the hall? It might be best if we spoke to him first. From what I've heard so far, the only two people with a possible motive are him and Sir Rodney."

"Why not speak to Sir Rodney first?"

"Is he still at the hall?"

Eliza shook her head. "No. They live in London and travelled back yesterday afternoon after the verdict."

"I'll speak to him when I go back then." Inspector Adams put a reminder in his notebook. "Just another thought. What about the women?"

"What about them?" Mr Bell said.

"What were their alibis? Has anyone considered the possibility of a woman being the murderer?"

Eliza shook her head. "Lord Beaufort dismissed us all on the grounds that we wouldn't have been strong enough to make such an impact in the skull with the mallet."

"And they were all titled ladies," Connie said. "We were the only ones there who weren't titled ... and Henry. It looks to us as if Lord Beaufort deliberately blamed Mr Bell to save his friends."

A frown crossed the inspector's face. "Did Lord Beaufort examine the body?"

"No, it was just us and Dr Thomson."

"And did Dr Thomson agree that the impact couldn't have been made by a woman?"

Eliza looked at Connie. "He didn't say one way or the other as I remember."

"No, he didn't. He just said the angle of the indent suggested the person who had swung the mallet was likely to have been shorter than Sir Cyril."

"Which would include all the ladies I imagine?"

"It would ... as well as Lord Lowton or Lord Albert," Eliza said.

"All right, let's not go over that again. On reflection, I think the first person I need to speak to is Lord Beaufort himself. He seems to have made some rather absurd assumptions and accepted a number of unconfirmed alibis. Let's see what he has to say before I go any further."

"Will we go this afternoon?"

Inspector Adams was about to respond when he stopped and stared at Eliza. "We?"

"Of course *we*. Lord Beaufort's already accused the wrong man and I need to know what's going on to make sure Father walks from here a free man."

CHAPTER FIFTEEN

Eliza and Connie climbed into the police carriage as Inspector Adams instructed the driver to take them to the home of Lord Beaufort.

"At least it's still the Easter recess for the House of Lords, so he should still be in Lowton rather than London," Eliza said as the carriage moved off.

Inspector Adams coughed to clear his throat. "You do realise that this visit is most irregular? I can't just take you into the man's home without getting permission. I have good reason to talk to him, but he has no obligation to let you in."

"I realise that, but might I suggest that if he refuses it implies he has something to hide?" Eliza eyed the inspector, who sat opposite her. "Perhaps mention that to him."

"Thank you, Mrs Thomson, I do know how to do my job."

"I'm sorry, of course you do, but ... well, not all police officers do."

A smile returned to Inspector Adams' face. "We're not all

rural bobbies with nothing to keep us busy except returning the occasional child to school."

Connie glared at Inspector Adams. "Not all rural bobbies are bad and you shouldn't suggest they are. We don't all want to live in London, you know, and Sergeant Cooper works very hard to keep Moreton safe."

"There you are, Inspector. A vote of confidence for one of your rural colleagues." Eliza couldn't keep the smirk from her face.

"I'm very glad to hear it, I'm sure he does." The inspector turned his attention to the view from the window as a large detached residence came into view. "It looks like we're here already. He's done nicely for himself, hasn't he?"

Eliza admired the three-storey, box-shaped house which extended out on both sides into the gardens. "I would say so. I knew he lived close to Lowton Hall, but I hadn't realised how close. You will do your best to get us in, won't you?"

Inspector Adams walked to the front door with Eliza and Connie close behind. An elderly man in formal dress answered the door.

"Inspector Adams from New Scotland Yard and two acquaintances to see His Lordship."

"Do you have an appointment, sir?"

"No, but if you could tell His Lordship it is rather urgent, I'd appreciate it." Inspector Adams gave his best smile.

The butler invited them into the hallway and asked them to wait as he disappeared to find Lord Beaufort.

"Very nice." Inspector Adams studied the walls decorated with red flock wallpaper that held an array of portraits.

"I don't suppose I'd complain, but compared to Lowton

Hall, it's not much. Perhaps that's why he spends so much time there." Eliza stepped forward to study a painting as the butler reappeared.

"His Lordship will receive you in his office." The butler spoke to Inspector Adams, but Eliza and Connie wasted no time following him as he was led to a room at the end of a short corridor.

Lord Beaufort stood up from behind an enormous polished desk. "Oh, it's you." His smile disappeared when he saw Eliza and Connie.

"Good afternoon, sir." Eliza gave a slight curtsey, before running her eyes over the mahogany wall panels and the magnificent fire surround to her right.

"Lord Beaufort, forgive us for disturbing you." Inspector Adams stepped forward and offered his hand across the desk. "I'm Inspector Adams from New Scotland Yard and I believe you know Mrs Thomson and Mrs Appleton."

"We have met." Lord Beaufort's eyes were like pinpricks as he glowered at Eliza. "What is it you want?"

"W-we'd like to talk to you." A shiver ran down Eliza's back at the force of Lord Beaufort's question.

"I hope you don't mind them joining us," the inspector said. "We need to ask you about the death of Sir Cyril Lowton and the inquest you held on Sunday afternoon."

Lord Beaufort leaned his hands on the desk and stared at each of them. "Before we start, Inspector, a question for you. Why are New Scotland Yard involved? Lord Lowton didn't alert you to the situation, and in fact gave strict instructions that the police shouldn't be troubled with the matter." Lord Beaufort's glare focussed on Eliza.

"You left me with no choice," Eliza said. "You held a

sham inquest on Sunday afternoon and concluded my father was guilty of murder. You said at the time it was because he was the only one not to have an alibi, but I've since learned he was about the only person in the house who did."

"Mrs Thomson, please." Inspector Adams held up his hand to quieten Eliza. "Lord Beaufort, Mrs Thomson alerted us to the case because she feels Mr Bell has been wrongly arrested. With the likelihood he'll be charged with Sir Cyril's murder, we have little choice but to get involved, not least because we need to make sure Mr Bell has a fair hearing. Mrs Thomson's taken me through some of the details, but obviously she wasn't present at the inquest. I hoped you'd share what you learned with us."

"This is most irregular." The skin of Lord Beaufort's neck wobbled as he shook his head. "You had no right to disobey Lord Lowton."

"The thing is," Inspector Adams said, "Mrs Thomson is acting on behalf of her father and so she needs to know what happened at the inquest. If you could tell her now, at the same time as you tell me, it would save me having to repeat it all."

Eliza thought she would shrivel up under Lord Beaufort's gaze, but eventually he sat down and beckoned for them to do likewise.

"Very well. What do you want to know?"

Inspector Adams cleared his throat. "Firstly, could you give us an overview of the proceedings and explain how you reached the conclusion you did?"

"I can assure you I reached my decision quite impartially."

"I'm sure you did, but you'll appreciate that as things

stand, Mr Bell faces the possibility of a death sentence. We need to make sure we have the right man."

"I hope you appreciate that Sir Cyril was a well-known society gentleman and there's bound to be plenty of interest in the case. Lord Lowton specifically said he wants the details kept out of the newspapers."

Inspector Adams nodded. "We'll try our best, but I ought to tell you we've alerted the coroner and it's likely he'll want to hold his own inquest. If you could go over the details with us beforehand, it may reduce the need for further questioning."

Lord Beaufort stood up and ambled to a large cabinet that stood in the corner behind his desk. After a minute, he returned to his seat with a thin wad of paper. "As you're aware, we held the inquest on Sunday afternoon and I interviewed all the guests who had stayed at the hall over the weekend. I asked each of them what they had been doing at the time of the death."

"And you told them that the time of death was about half past ten on the Saturday morning?" Inspector Adams said.

"Not exactly. I always like to find out a little about what they did before and afterwards and so I asked what they'd been doing between ten and eleven that morning. As you would expect from such a distinguished guest list, the lords and ladies of the house were all busy, either in each other's company or helping with the arrangements for the ball."

"And there was nobody without an alibi?"

"The only two gentlemen whose whereabouts no one could vouch for were Sir Rodney and Mr Bell. Clearly, as a knight of His Majesty's realm, Sir Rodney is above suspicion. Mr Bell, on the other hand, was not only found to have an incomplete alibi, he had the motive and was at the scene of the crime."

Eliza could hold her tongue no longer. "You can't send my father to the gallows just because he was the only man without a title."

"My dear, have you not been listening? That is not the reason I found him guilty." Lord Beaufort looked back at his notes. "Yes, here it is. Not only was he at the scene of the crime, he had the murder weapon in his hand, which he tried to hide before anyone could examine it. Fortunately Lord Lowton found it under the bushes."

"Lord Lowton found it...?" Eliza stopped and turned to the inspector but he interrupted her.

"Mrs Thomson, please. Let me do the talking. Lord Beaufort, Mr Bell said he called for help as soon as he found the body. Why would he do that if he was the murderer? Surely it would have been more sensible to keep quiet until the surrounding area was clear?"

"The man obviously panicked and called out without realising it."

Inspector Adams nodded. "So tell me, why did you discount the interview with Sir Rodney? I heard he was walking alone in the grounds and nobody can confirm that he's telling the truth."

"And being a knight of the realm is not a good enough reason." Eliza glared at him.

Lord Beaufort sat unflustered as he addressed the inspector. "It was quite simple really, he was nowhere near the scene at the time of the incident."

"But you only have his word for it?" Inspector Adams said.

"That, Inspector, is good enough for me. Besides, what reason would he have for murdering Sir Cyril?"

Inspector Adams turned back to his notes. "Perhaps the fact that Sir Cyril constantly belittled his daughter and taunted her about not being good enough for the family. I understand he had been particularly vicious on Friday evening and maybe Sir Rodney decided enough was enough."

"We have no evidence to suggest anything of the sort. Mr Bell, on the other hand, was heard complaining about Sir Cyril over breakfast on the morning of the murder." He turned his attention to Eliza. "When I interviewed you, you even confirmed he'd been in the garden with you and Mrs Appleton but had left you in order to 'have a word' with Sir Cyril. Five minutes later, Sir Cyril was found dead. Don't tell me that's a coincidence."

Eliza's face flushed. "That's because Father found him, not because he killed him."

"Mrs Thomson, please, let me deal with this." Inspector Adams' face was stern. "We're here today to find out what Lord Beaufort learned during the investigation, not question it. Forgive me, Your Lordship. Can you tell me how many of the other alibis were confirmed?"

"Most of them, I would say. I was with Lord Lowton in his office on the morning in question, Lord Forsyth was in the snooker room waiting for the younger gentlemen, and the ladies were either helping with the preparations for the ball or keeping each other company."

Inspector Adams nodded as he finished writing in his notebook. "One point about that. You said that you and Lord Lowton were in the office between ten and eleven, but we know he was by the lake at around half past ten when the body was found. Did it occur to you to question that?"

"We were together before he walked to the lake."

"But not for the full hour. Did he explain how he was on the scene of the crime so quickly? I'm not familiar with the layout of Lowton Hall, but I understand it would normally take fifteen to twenty minutes to walk from the house to the edge of the lake."

Lord Beaufort shuffled the papers on his desk and prepared to stand up. "He left shortly before the incident to inspect the lawn. They've had moles, you know, and he wanted to see if the traps they'd set were working."

"So his alibi's worthless." Eliza struggled to keep her voice level.

"His alibi is perfectly acceptable. There wouldn't possibly have been time for him to murder anyone between him leaving the office and the reported time of death."

"So what time did he leave you?" Inspector Adams asked.

Lord Beaufort huffed as he peered at the clock. "It was turned ten o'clock."

"Can you be more precise?"

Lord Beaufort stood up from his desk. "At least quarter past ... now, I really must be going."

"Thank you, Your Lordship, we'll confirm that with Lord Lowton when we speak to him."

Lord Beaufort stopped where he was. "You can't question Lord Lowton."

Inspector Adams cocked his head to one side. "We need to ask him about his brother and the fact he was on the scene when the body was discovered. It's routine."

"I still won't have you speaking to him without me being present."

"You act as if he has something to hide." Eliza spoke with the most controlled voice she could muster.

"Nonsense, but I will not have the police or anyone else asking him inappropriate questions."

With another glare at Eliza, Inspector Adams continued. "Do you know if anyone saw him in the garden? It would help support his alibi if they did."

"I'm sure somebody will have done. One of the gardeners, perhaps. I'll speak to our estate manager and get him to ask around."

"Very well and if you could give us the names of anyone we should speak to, that would be helpful." Inspector Adams reviewed his notes. "Just to let you know, there are a few other points we need clarifying and so we'll talk to all the guests again as well as Lady Victoria and her children. I believe you excluded them from the initial investigation."

"You can't disturb Lady Victoria. She's in deep mourning."

"Again, purely routine. We'll also speak to Lord Forsyth before we talk to Lord Lowton. He's in London, I believe, and so we'll travel over there tomorrow and call on Sir Rodney while we're there. I doubt we'll get to Lowton Hall before Wednesday afternoon. If you'd care to join us, you're more than welcome."

CHAPTER SIXTEEN

T he following morning, the clock in the hall struck ten as Eliza and Connie walked down the stairs in time to see Soams open the door to Inspector Adams.

"Good morning, ladies. It's a lovely day for a drive to Richmond." The inspector removed his hat as he stepped though the doorway.

"Good morning, Inspector. I trust you were comfortable in the boarding house." Eliza smiled when she saw him.

"It was ... adequate." He glanced at the extensive chandelier hanging above the central staircase in the hall. "We can't all live a life of luxury. Are you ready to go?"

"We are. We've been up since seven and taken some breakfast to father. I don't want him wasting away while he's in that cell. Do you want to lead the way?"

The carriage didn't hurry as it followed the meandering banks of the River Thames for several miles before crossing the river and heading towards the tree-lined streets of Richmond.

"Are we going to see Sir Rodney first?" Connie asked.

"We are, we'll go to the Forsyths' later. Do you know which house we want?" The inspector studied the address in his hand as they turned into the street they were looking for.

Eliza rested a finger on her lips as she peered through the window. "It's a few years since I was last here, but I think it's further down on the left. It's a large detached house. Double-fronted if I remember rightly."

The inspector let out a low whistle. "All the houses around here are big. Did it come with the knighthood?"

Eliza chuckled. "It was more like the knighthood came with it. Once you can afford one of these, people start taking notice of you. Father has one in the next street."

"Hence his invite to Lowton Hall?"

Eliza shook her head. "Not quite, although he was keen to meet Lord Lowton. No, Father's been friendly with Sir Rodney since he was plain Mr Brough. They both had businesses making components for the railways and when Caroline was born, Father was asked to be her godfather."

"So this friendship goes back a long way?"

"It does and Sir Rodney's such a nice man, I don't believe he would harm Sir Cyril and let Father take the blame for it." Eliza pointed ahead to a large four-storey house. "There it is, the one with the black-and-white front door. Let's hope he has some information for us."

Having received a telegram from Inspector Adams the previous evening, Sir Rodney and Lady Rosemary were waiting for them in the hallway.

"Oh, my dear–" Lady Rosemary put an arm around Eliza's shoulders "–how's Mr Bell? It was such a terrible shock to see him led away like that."

Eliza sighed. "As you can imagine, he's felt better, but he knows we're trying to help."

"Terrible business, this whole thing," Sir Rodney said. "Come on through to the morning room and let's see if we can help."

Eliza and Connie accepted matching armchairs near the window and waited while Lady Rosemary poured the tea and offered around a selection of biscuits. Once she'd finished fussing, she sat on the settee beside Sir Rodney allowing Inspector Adams the chance to speak.

"Lady Rosemary, at the time of the incident, am I right in thinking you were in the marquee helping your daughter with the arrangements for the ball?"

"I was, Inspector. We were in there all day, weren't we, Rodney?"

"All day, m'dear, you were exhausted when you came to dress for dinner."

"Exhausted, that's right, dear."

"And so while you were in the marquee, did you see Sir Cyril at all, or any of the other male guests?"

"Gracious no, it was only women in there. I don't think we saw a man all day, oh, except for the men who came to move the tables. Hired helps, you know the sort of chaps."

"How many of them were there?"

The question flustered Lady Rosemary. "Oh, I'm sure I couldn't say. They were in and out, possibly six, or maybe ten. Caroline would know."

"Very good, my lady, I'll make a note to ask her." He leaned forward in his seat to write in his notebook before turning to Sir Rodney. "And so, sir, if I can assume you weren't in the marquee on Saturday, may I ask what you were doing?"

"Indeed you can. I was out in the gardens taking a walk. I went straight after breakfast when Rosemary disappeared with Caroline. No point hanging around the house on your own on a day like that I thought."

"Yes, quite." Inspector Adams failed to suppress a smile. "Can you tell me where you walked?"

"I was in the formal gardens at the back of the house, not far from George and the ladies, if you must know. They were on the other side to me and slightly ahead, and so when I got to the point where the path crosses the lawn I upped my step and tried to catch them."

"By George you mean Mr Bell?" the inspector asked.

"Yes, yes, of course. He was the only George there that weekend. I think he must have known I was after him though because no sooner had I started on the path across the lawn than he raised his hat to the ladies and headed off towards the glorious rhododendron bushes. They looked magnificent with their mix of pale and shocking pink flowers. Did you see them, m'dear?" He was talking again to Lady Rosemary, but Inspector Adams interrupted.

"So did you catch up with him?"

"Well, no, but perhaps I should have done. The problem is, Neville doesn't like anyone walking on the lawn and so with George heading in the opposite direction, it would have taken me too long to go all the way around. That was when I stopped to consider my options. I was about to go back to my original route when I saw Neville heading towards the lake from the right-hand path."

"You saw Lord Lowton?" Eliza said. "When would this have been? Was it when Father was still by the bushes?"

Sir Rodney paused to think. "I suppose it must have been around the same time."

"And so did you go back and join him?" Inspector Adams asked.

"Good gracious, no. Why would I do that? I'd already told him to speak to Sir Cyril about the way he treated Caroline and so I put my head down and hoped he hadn't seen me."

"You spoke to Lord Lowton about Sir Cyril?"

"I most certainly did." Sir Rodney's face coloured. "I was tired of Sir Cyril treating Caroline the way he did, and..."

"And what?" Eliza said.

Sir Rodney squirmed in his chair. "I'm really not sure I should mention this, but I'd overheard an argument on the Saturday morning between Neville and Sir Cyril."

"An argument? What time was this?"

"Oh, I couldn't tell you exactly, but it was when I was on my way for breakfast. Rosemary had gone ahead of me to meet Caroline and as I walked past Neville's office, the door was ajar. It was a private conversation."

A chill ran down Eliza's back. "Could you tell us what it was about? It might be important."

Sir Rodney wiped his forehead with a handkerchief. "Well, yes, I suppose so. It was all Sir Cyril, really. He was bawling at Neville, accusing him of lowering the standards of the family by marrying Caroline and–" Sir Rodney took a deep breath "–forgive me for saying this, but he accused Caroline of bringing her common friends and acquaintances to the house."

"You mean us!" Connie put a hand to her chest.

Eliza grimaced. "I imagine that's exactly what Sir Cyril meant."

Sir Rodney nodded. "Yes, I fear it was, but it wasn't just directed at you, it was us as well. I must admit when I arrived for breakfast I was angry with Sir Cyril, very angry in fact."

"He was." Lady Rosemary nodded vigorously. "As angry as I've seen him."

"Was that why you went into the garden then, to look for him?" Inspector Adams asked.

Sir Rodney's cheeks wobbled as he shook his head. "Not at all, I wouldn't have confronted him. He was Caroline's brother-in-law, and I didn't want to make life any more difficult for her. I knew the only person he would take any notice of was Neville and so I had a quiet word."

"And you think that was where Lord Lowton was heading when you saw him, to speak to Sir Cyril?"

Sir Rodney shrugged. "It's hard to tell. They were approaching the lake from opposite directions and may not even have known the other was there. I only noticed Sir Cyril by the bushes when I saw George leaving the ladies. He headed straight for Sir Cyril but he'd disappeared before George reached him."

"And you didn't follow them?"

"I did not, they were the last people I wanted to see. No, I kept walking and headed for the left-hand side of the lake where the trees would shield me from their view."

Eliza nodded. "Can you be more precise about the time you saw Lord Lowton? Could you say whether it was before or after half past ten?"

Sir Rodney paused. "Let me think. If I remember

correctly, it was a minute or two before the clock on the front of the house struck the half hour."

Eliza's brow furrowed as she turned to Connie. "Where were we when the clock struck? I didn't hear it."

Connie screwed up her forehead. "I don't know, I don't think I heard it either."

"You were still on the left-hand footpath," Sir Rodney said. "It was just before you turned to follow George."

"So all the men were ahead of us even before Father shouted?"

Sir Rodney shrugged. "I didn't hear him call but if you were near the bushes when he did, then yes."

Inspector Adams looked up from his notebook. "When you saw Lord Lowton and Sir Cyril, did you notice if either was carrying a croquet mallet?"

Sir Rodney scratched his head. "Now you're asking. Neville certainly didn't have one. He was walking in his usual manner with his arms swinging by his sides as if he were still on military parade. Sir Cyril, on the other hand, I really can't say. I seem to remember he was partially hidden by the bushes and so maybe he did. I couldn't swear to it though."

"I still think it would be strange for Sir Cyril to take the murder weapon to the lake," Connie said.

"Perhaps he was planning on doing something else with it and the murderer seized it from him?" Sir Rodney said. "It's probably not so unusual."

Connie frowned. "I suppose not, but it could mean we're still looking for someone else."

Eliza nodded before turning back to Sir Rodney. "Was

there anyone else outside while you were walking, especially near the croquet lawn if you went that way?"

"Not really, not to speak to at any rate. I did see Lady Victoria walking back to the house with Lord David, although from the way they were walking it didn't look like they were out for a stroll."

"Lady Victoria? Was that before or after you saw us?"

"Now then, it would have been after I saw you. They were on the right-hand path where I'd originally started but they must have walked behind me as I took the path across the centre of the lawn. They were almost at the house by the time I saw them."

"So they must have seen Lord Lowton?"

Sir Rodney shrugged. "Possibly, although he'd disappeared from view by the time I saw them and I'm not exactly sure where they'd come from."

"What about Lord Albert?" Connie asked. "Did you see him approach the bushes?"

Sir Rodney shook his head. "No, I didn't see him at all that morning. Why?"

"We know he was on the scene of the crime very quickly after Father called out," Eliza said. "The problem is, we haven't confirmed where he came from."

Connie cocked her head to one side. "Could it have been him with the croquet mallet?"

"Are you suggesting my grandson's the killer?" Sir Rodney's expression changed. "That's ludicrous."

"Of course it wasn't him." Lady Rosemary wailed. "How could you even think that?"

Connie put a hand to her lips. "Oh my goodness, no I'm not saying that, I'm so sorry."

Inspector Adams glared at Connie. "We're not suggesting anything at the moment, we're just gathering information. Please don't be alarmed. Now, is there anything else you can tell us?"

Lady Rosemary wiped her eyes with a handkerchief. "I wish there was, Inspector, especially if it proved the innocence of my grandson, but I just can't help."

"Don't worry, m'dear." Sir Rodney patted his wife's hand. "I'm sure the inspector will work it out."

"I certainly hope so, sir." Inspector Adams stood up. "Now, we really must be going. Thank you for seeing us. If you think of anything else of relevance, please let one of us know."

The carriage was waiting for them at the end of the drive when the butler showed them out and they hurried to take their seats.

"What do we think of that?" Eliza asked as they pulled away from the kerb. "It proves Lord Lowton was near the lake before Sir Cyril was murdered."

"It would certainly seem so."

"You don't look very pleased about it, though," Connie said.

Inspector Adams shook his head. "I'd really rather not have Lord Lowton as a suspect. It would make life so much easier if the butler did it."

Eliza giggled. "Poor Soams, you can't go blaming him. I bet he was rushed off his feet all day running errands for Caroline."

The inspector sighed. "I'm sure you're right, but it's not

straightforward if you want to arrest an earl. There are procedures to follow."

"Well, I'm sure we'll manage them if we must."

"It was interesting to hear about Lady Victoria and her son," Connie said. "Lord Beaufort didn't interview them because she's the grieving widow."

"And probably because she's the daughter of an earl," Eliza added.

"Well, from where we were sitting she didn't seem to do much grieving on Saturday night," Connie said.

"What do you mean?" the inspector asked.

"I mean that the ball was only a matter of hours after Lord Lowton told her of Sir Cyril's death and yet she was all smiles and on very good terms with a man Lady Rosemary suggested was the estate manager."

Inspector Adams frowned. "I wonder why Lady Rosemary didn't say anything about that when we were interviewing her."

Eliza sighed. "I suppose we asked the wrong questions. We only focussed on the time of the murder."

Connie's eyes lit up. "Do you think she could have been to see the estate manager when Sir Rodney saw her?"

"I doubt it," Eliza said. "Especially if she had her son with her."

"He may have disturbed them."

Inspector Adams took out his notebook. "I suppose we'd better speak to this estate manager. We'll be back in Lowton tomorrow and should have time before we talk to His Lordship."

"Or after," Connie said.

Inspector Adams grimaced. "That's if we're not escorted

off the premises. The likes of Lord Lowton don't take kindly to being questioned, especially if they don't like the questions."

"Surely that would be an admission of guilt?" Eliza said.

"It almost always means they know something they don't want to tell us, that's for sure."

"We'll need an early start then," Eliza said. "We'd better get a move on if we want to talk to the Forsyths this afternoon. It's more important than ever we talk to them given they sat with Lady Victoria and her 'friend' at the ball. Perhaps they could answer a few questions about him."

CHAPTER SEVENTEEN

They stopped off at a tavern for a bite to eat, before Inspector Adams directed the driver to an address in Kensington. Thirty minutes later, they pulled up outside a four-storey, double-fronted town house, within walking distance of Kensington Palace.

"I bet Sir Cyril hated coming here," Eliza said as she admired the cream render on the front walls. "I imagine it really made him feel unimportant compared to each of his siblings."

Connie laughed. "Didn't you say the other sister married a marquess as well? They probably have an even more prestigious London address."

"Not to mention their country mansions, while poor Sir Cyril had to live in a cottage." Eliza laughed.

"Well, let's hope they're in residence," the inspector said. "If they've so many houses, they may not be in."

"I'm sure they'll be in. We're at the start of the debutante season when the whole set move to London. Lady Hilda's presenting her niece to the King, she'll want to be local."

"Yes, of course, how could I forget?" The inspector's mouth twisted as he headed for the front door.

The butler showed them into a large wood-panelled drawing room with matching wooden beams. Despite the fine weather, a fire roared in the grate while Lady Hilda reclined on a chaise longue that sat neatly within the confines of the bay window.

"I thought this was all over and done with," she said without moving. "Lord Beaufort sorted it out for us. What happened to the chap they arrested?"

Eliza took a deep breath. "The chap they arrested, Mr Bell, is my father, and he did not murder Sir Cyril."

"Well, I think you'll find Lord Beaufort has the evidence to show he did."

Eliza was about to respond, but a glance from Inspector Adams stopped her.

"Lady Forsyth, in a case such as this, the police need to be involved before it goes to court. If he's found guilty, Mr Bell would face the death penalty and so we need to make sure we have the right man."

"Does Lord Beaufort know you're questioning his verdict?"

Inspector Adams flashed his best smile. "We've spoken with him, of course, and gone through his evidence, but we have a few further questions, if you don't mind."

Lady Hilda squirmed in her seat. "I suppose I can spare a few minutes, although I doubt my husband can. He's frightfully busy at the moment."

"We asked the butler to see if he could join us. I'm sure he'll understand."

Lady Hilda scowled at them as they stood in an awkward

semicircle around her. "Very well, what do you want to know?"

"First of all, can you confirm where you were between ten and eleven o'clock last Saturday?"

"I'm sure Lord Beaufort's note would tell you I was in the conservatory with Lady Victoria."

"Lady Victoria?" The words were out of Eliza's mouth before she could stop them.

"Yes, my sister-in-law and Sir Cyril's wife, or should I say–" she dabbed at her eyes with a handkerchief "–his widow."

"Yes, of course, I'm just surprised Lord Beaufort accepted your alibi given he didn't question Lady Victoria. Was there someone else who confirmed your whereabouts?"

"I imagine so. Lady Beaufort always seems to follow us around and so I'm sure she would oblige."

When Inspector Adams didn't look up from his notebook Eliza continued.

"Talking of Lady Victoria, I saw she attended the ball on Saturday evening, despite the news."

"One has appearances to keep up, of course she was there."

Eliza pursed her lips. "I see. I wonder, can you tell us about the gentleman she was with? I don't believe he was one of the weekend guests."

"She wasn't with anyone in particular. She'd just lost her husband and was being sociable with everyone."

"Forgive me, I didn't mean to imply any wrongdoing, but there was one man who caught my eye. He was tall with broad shoulders and a dark complexion."

Lady Hilda took a deep breath as she regarded Eliza. "Yes, I remember him, but I don't recall his name."

"That's a pity." Inspector Adams finally looked up. "Never mind, we can ask Lady Victoria when we speak to her tomorrow."

Eliza saw the panic in Lady Hilda's eyes.

"You'll speak to Victoria, after everything she's been through? How could you?"

"Sir Cyril was her husband and we need to know if she saw anything unusual," Inspector Adams said.

"Of course she didn't, she was in the conservatory with me. At least Lord Beaufort had the sense to realise that."

Eliza watched the inspector as he flicked though his notebook. *Come on, man, ask the question if you don't want me to.*

Inspector Adams found the page he was looking for and gave a nervous cough. "Can you tell me what time she joined you?"

"Immediately after breakfast."

"I see." The inspector rubbed his chin. "The thing is, we have it on good authority that Lady Victoria was seen in the gardens at around half past ten, which would mean she couldn't have been in the conservatory. At least not for the whole hour."

Lady Hilda visibly froze.

"Would you care to be more precise about when she was with you?"

Lady Hilda reached for her fan and wafted it around her face. "W-we walked to the conservatory together from breakfast."

"With Lady Beaufort following you?" Eliza said.

"Yes ... no ... I don't remember, she may have been a little later."

"But Lady Victoria didn't stay long before she left to go into the garden?"

"She needed to find Lord David and only went outside for a few minutes."

"But those minutes just happened to coincide with the murder of her husband?" Eliza's voice sounded triumphant.

"I hope you're not implying Lady Victoria would murder my brother. Lord Beaufort was clearly a step ahead of you when he realised the dent in my brother's head was so severe that it couldn't possibly have been made by a lady."

Inspector Adams once again put up his hand. "Please. We haven't yet confirmed whether the wound could have been caused by a lady, but even if it was, it wouldn't stop her seeing something that may be relevant."

"Was it true that Lady Victoria and Sir Cyril often argued?" Connie asked.

"Argued? What gave you that idea?"

"It was just something Lady Caroline said on the Friday night before dinner. Lady Victoria wanted a second drink and Lady Caroline wondered why."

"Of course they didn't argue, no more than any other couple at any rate. Caroline really needs to keep these things to herself."

Eliza raised an eyebrow to Connie as the door to the drawing room opened and Lord Forsyth joined them.

Inspector Adams turned and extended his hand towards him. "Thank you so much for joining us, sir. We'll only take a few minutes of your time."

"That's quite all right, Inspector. Always happy to help."

"Excellent, well, let me see. I understand from Lord Beaufort that between ten and eleven o'clock on the day of the murder, you were in the snooker room waiting for your nephews and their friend."

"Yes, that's right. Half past ten we'd agreed to meet and the little blighters didn't turn up. Damned inconvenient."

"And so were you in the room on your own?"

"Soams stuck his head around the door, I would say at about a quarter past ten to ask if I wanted anything, which unfortunately I didn't. Had I asked for a pot of tea he could have provided my alibi, but as it was, nobody can vouch for my whereabouts at half past."

"Did any of the boys ever arrive at the snooker room?" Eliza asked.

"Lord David did, probably at about a quarter to eleven. He said he'd been reading and hadn't realised the time." Lord Forsyth paused. "Neither Albert nor his friend turned up though. They didn't even send their apologies."

"Did that strike you as odd?" Inspector Adams asked.

"I can't speak for the friend, I'd only met him briefly on the Friday evening, but yes, it was unusual for Albert to be inconsiderate."

"So, did you ask him where he'd been when you did eventually see him?"

Lord Forsyth shook his head. "I didn't see him again until we heard the news of Cyril's death and suddenly such a petty incident seemed irrelevant. You don't think he had anything to do with it, do you?"

"Don't be absurd." Lady Hilda waved a hand at her husband. "Why on earth would Albert want Cyril dead?"

Lord Forsyth nodded. "She has a point, no sense in it at all."

"So you weren't aware of any quarrels between Sir Cyril and anyone else in the family?" Eliza asked.

Lord Forsyth threw back his head as a laugh burst from his lungs. "Cyril quarrelled with everyone, but we were all used to him, certainly no one would kill him for it. No, if you ask me, the chap Beaufort had arrested was the most likely culprit. Not used to Cyril, you see. Didn't know when to ignore him."

Eliza's mouth dropped open as she stared at Lord Forsyth.

"If that's all you need, I'll be off." Lord Forsyth walked to the door. "If you think of anything else, you can always write to me. We'll be here until August."

Eliza was in a daze as the butler showed them out and once they were on the footpath, she stopped and scowled at Inspector Adams.

"Did you believe him?"

"Well ... it's too early to say."

"You did, didn't you? He nearly had us all fooled. All the way through I was thinking what a nice man he was, and how easy it was for Lord Beaufort to accept his alibi even though he had no one to confirm it, but can't you tell he was lying?" Eliza turned to Connie for support. "The whole thing was scripted, designed to make us believe Father was the murderer."

Connie hesitated. "Could he be the killer?"

Eliza shook her head. "No, I don't think so, but I would say he's hiding something ... and as for his wife..."

"That was my thought," Inspector Adams said. "I don't

know about Lord Forsyth, but Lady Hilda didn't want us finding out about Lady Victoria, or anyone else come to think of it."

Eliza pursed her lips. "That would explain why she was upset that Caroline mentioned that Sir Cyril and Lady Victoria often argued."

"I can't say I'm familiar with the ways of our ruling classes, but from what I've heard I'd say they like to keep their dirty little secrets to themselves, away from the prying eyes of us commoners. My guess is, they want to keep this out of the newspapers at all costs and they're prepared to do whatever they need to."

"So what do we do now?" Connie asked. "If Lord Forsyth's alibi was pre-prepared, maybe they've agreed on what they should all say."

"It's quite possible and I'm beginning to feel rather uneasy about things," Inspector Adams said. "I think I need to speak to my superiors about this. They know I'm working on a murder case, but I haven't told them who the victim is or the suspects. If we decide Lord Lowton or any one of the others is guilty, I can't just barge in and arrest them without the permission of the chief constable, or possibly the Home Secretary. Heaven help us if Lord Beaufort's in on it."

"But we can't stop now!" Eliza's voice pierced the air. "Wouldn't it be better to gather all the evidence first before you tell them? Then you can get an arrest warrant for the right person."

Inspector Adams kicked at several loose stones on the edge of the kerb.

"Please. We only have the Lowtons and Lady Victoria to

speak to. Can't you give us one more day?" Eliza thought time had stopped before Inspector Adams nodded.

"One more day. We just have to hope that Lord Lowton doesn't put in a complaint about us before I get back to London."

"Will you travel back to Lowton with us now?"

The inspector stared into the distance in the direction of Central London before nodding. "I will. Who could resist another night in that boarding house?"

CHAPTER EIGHTEEN

Inspector Adams dropped Eliza and Connie off at the front door of Lowton Hall with a promise to pick them up at nine o'clock the following morning. By the time they'd watched him pull away, Soams was holding the front door open for them.

"Good evening, ladies." He gave his customary bow as they approached the steps. "We were about to clear away the afternoon tea dishes. Would you care for anything before we do?"

"A cup of tea would be lovely," Eliza said. "We won't take up much of your time."

Soams led them to the drawing room where he checked the water levels in the teapot and ordered a maid to bring a fresh batch of cakes. Eliza waited for him to leave before she approached a tall, dark-haired young man slouching in a chair overlooking the garden.

"Good afternoon, Henry."

Henry jumped to his feet, his eyes wide. "Mother, what are you doing here? I thought you'd left."

Eliza turned to his companion who sat on the chair opposite. "Good afternoon, Lord Albert. I hope you don't mind but I'd like a word with Henry. Would you excuse us for a minute?" She linked Henry's arm and directed him towards the door. "We can talk upstairs. I'll ask Soams to bring the tea up there."

Henry glanced between the two women as Eliza shut the door to their private lounge area.

"You seem to be going to great lengths to avoid me at the moment," Eliza said.

"No ... not at all, I thought you'd gone home on Sunday like everyone else."

"You mean when you were supposed to be travelling with me? We searched everywhere for you when your father was leaving and could find no trace of you. I thought you wanted to speak to him."

"I did, but ... I was busy and didn't realise the time. I thought you'd left together."

"Busy?" Eliza couldn't keep the sarcasm from her voice. "A weekend guest at a place like this is never busy, only preoccupied. I hope it wasn't with Lady Alice..."

"No, of course not." At the mention of Lady Alice, Henry's face coloured, and he turned his attention to the pattern on the carpet.

"Don't lie to me, Henry Thomson."

"I'm not..."

"Yes, you are, I can always tell. What is the matter with you? You've been told more than once this weekend, including by Lord Lowton himself, to stay away from Lady Alice and yet you persist in spending time with her."

"We're just friends."

"I don't care whether you're friends or not, you have no right to spend time with her, especially not alone. Anything could happen."

"Don't be silly, we just enjoy walking around the grounds together."

"If you must spend time with her, you should at least have a chaperone. Lord Albert likes to walk, do you ever ask him to join you?"

"Sometimes." Henry wandered over to the window.

"Well, I'm telling you one final time, I do not want to see or hear that you've been alone with that young lady. She has her future mapped out and whether you like it or not, you are not part of it."

Henry spun around to face Eliza. "Do you realise how unhappy she is about it? She hasn't had any say in the plans."

"For someone like Lady Alice, that is beside the point. She is the daughter of an earl and they expect her to marry someone of her own class, preferably with a title and estate of their own. You can't hope to compete."

"Her father didn't marry in his own class. She told me her mother used to be one of us."

"And have you any idea how much trouble that's caused over the years. She's still not accepted in the way she should be. Lord Lowton's well aware of that and I imagine he's determined to make sure Lord Albert and Lady Alice marry appropriately."

Henry let out a sarcastic laugh. "He'll be lucky. Albert's already met someone at Cambridge who he's fallen for. Somebody else just like us. He told his father about her when we arrived on Friday afternoon and said there was nothing he could do to stop him marrying her. Not given the way Lord Lowton had married Lady Caroline."

Eliza paused as the words sank in and a moment later Soams knocked on the door with their tea.

"Just leave it there, thank you. We'll pour it ourselves," Eliza said.

Soams bowed and backed out of the door.

"I don't care what Lord Albert does," Eliza said when they were alone again. "You're my son and I'm telling you to stay away from Lady Alice. Have I made myself clear?"

Henry gave an unconvincing nod. "May I go now?"

"No, you can't. Do you have any recollection of the fact that your grandfather was arrested on Sunday afternoon? Aren't you even going to ask how he is?"

"How is he?" The petulance in his voice stung Eliza.

"Can't you show a bit more interest? Unsurprisingly, he's not happy. How would you feel if someone had accused you of a murder you didn't commit? He could face the gallows, has that even occurred to you?"

"So that's why you're still here? You think Grandfather's innocent and you're playing the detective trying to prove it?"

Eliza marched to the window and pulled on Henry's arm, forcing him to face her. "What has got into you? You used to love Grandfather and now you're mocking him."

"It's the way you go about it. Like last year, you had to play detective then, it's not right."

"Why is it not right?"

"Because women don't do things like that. You should leave it to the police."

Eliza's eyes fixed Henry where he was. "Is that what this is about? You don't think I should try to help Grandfather?

For your information, last year I proved that Sam Wilson was innocent of the murder charge the police had placed on him. If it hadn't been for me, he would have lost his life."

"It wasn't down to you. The police from New Scotland Yard were involved, you just like to think you're more important than you are and frankly it's embarrassing."

Eliza took a step backwards before turning to Connie.

"That's not true." Connie stood up and walked towards Henry. "The police would never have worked it out without your mother. She deserves credit, not criticism."

Eliza straightened her shoulders. "And if you think I'm going to sit around and let the police hang Grandfather, just to save your embarrassment, you can think again."

"Lord Beaufort's already conducted the inquiry. I was hardly delighted that Grandfather was arrested, but we have to move on. If he's the killer, he deserves justice."

"So you're just going to accept that he's guilty, after everything he's done for you? Doesn't he mean anything to you?"

"Oh course he does, but if he's innocent, you should tell the police."

"We already have. They're looking into it but we're helping out."

"You're hindering more like and poor Mrs Appleton gets dragged along just to keep you company."

"That's not true, I enjoy it." The tone of Connie's voice appeared to surprise Henry.

"The only person around here who's an embarrassment is you," Eliza said. "I don't know what's got into you."

Henry's shoulders slumped. "I just want a normal mother. Why can't you stay at home like everyone else's?"

"Because I'm not like most other women. Why is that so hard to understand?"

Henry shrugged. "It just doesn't seem right."

"Neither do all these murders. I don't choose to be around when they happen but if I am, I'm not going to sit around and do nothing. Not if I can help. Now come along, let's not argue. What did you want to speak to your father about?"

"Nothing."

"So you wanted to travel to Moreton for nothing?" Eliza paced across the room before turning back to face her son. "You want more money, don't you?"

Henry's eyes were pleading. "I don't need much."

"Well, however much you want, you're going to have to do some work for it."

"Work?"

"Yes, something you won't be familiar with, but Mrs Appleton and I need help with this case and you're going to give it to us if you want any money."

"What do I know about it?"

"That's what we'll find out. Seeing you'll be here for another few days and have access to Lord Albert, I want to know what you can find out from him."

"I can't tell tales on my friend."

Eliza pursed her lips and counted to three. "I won't listen to any more of this. Since when was Lord Albert more important than your grandfather?" When Henry failed to answer, Eliza continued. "We know he was walking around the lake on the morning of the murder, but what we don't know is why he was there when Lord Forsyth was expecting him, and you for that matter, in the snooker room. Why wasn't he there? And why was he so close to the scene of the crime?"

"He said he was going there to meet someone," Henry said. "He told me he wouldn't be long and to wait for him by the east wing."

"And so you waited with Lady Alice?"

"We sat together on the bench near the library but Albert didn't arrive."

"And Lady Alice didn't know who he was waiting for?"

Henry shook his head. "I don't think so, although when I suggested we go and find him she wouldn't because she said she'd get her shoes dirty."

Eliza paused. *Is there any significance in that?* After a moment she shook her head. "All right then, here's what I want you to do. I want you to try and find out who he met and also keep an eye open for anything that seems out of the ordinary. We'll be here until at least this time tomorrow and so as soon as afternoon tea is over, I want you up here again. Is that clear?"

Henry nodded. "I suppose so."

"Good. Your grandfather won't be held in Lowton police station for much longer and I want him freed before they send him to London. We've been to see him each morning, and he knows we're trying to help. If you find any information that could be useful, there may be a nice reward in it for you."

Eliza finally saw the hint of a smile on Henry's face. "Off you go and see what you can find out."

CHAPTER NINETEEN

Inspector Adams was waiting for them in the carriage by the time Eliza and Connie stepped outside the following morning.

"Good morning, Inspector," Eliza said. "You're keen today."

"I've made an appointment with Lord Lowton for two o'clock this afternoon and we need to see Lady Victoria in good time. I'd like to go over all the evidence before we see him."

"At least she lives on the estate, and so it shouldn't take us long to get there," Connie said.

Five minutes later, the carriage pulled up outside a large, three-storey, detached property.

"I thought she lived in a cottage," Connie said. "It's bigger than a whole row of cottages in Moreton."

"I suppose size is all relative," Eliza said. "It's bigger than anything we're used to, but it's smaller than the west wing of Lowton Hall. That must have annoyed Sir Cyril."

"They've still got a butler." Connie nodded towards the

front door, which was opened by a man in a formal black tailcoat.

Once they'd climbed down from the carriage Inspector Adams led the way and raised his hat as he approached the front door. "Good morning. Would it be possible to speak to Lady Lowton and her son, Lord David?"

"I'm afraid Lord David's out at the moment, but I'll speak to Her Ladyship and ask if she's able to receive you." The butler gave a bow before he closed the door, leaving them to wait outside.

"We need to ask the butler to send for Lord David before we go in," Inspector Adams said. "We haven't got time to come back."

Several minutes later, the door reopened and after taking their hats and coats the butler escorted them to the drawing room.

"Her Ladyship will see you in here. She'll join you presently."

"It's not quite as fancy as the Forsyths' house," Connie said.

Eliza ran her eyes around the wood-panelled walls covered with numerous family portraits. "Sir Cyril still liked to remember the family line though. It must be unnerving having all these eyes looking down at you."

"Especially when there's such a family resemblance," Connie added.

Hearing a click from the door, Eliza turned around as Lady Victoria stepped into the room, the black fabric of her mourning clothes heightening the paleness of her skin and blonde hair.

Inspector Adams stared at her, his mouth open.

"Forgive us for intruding at such a difficult time." Unsure what else to do, Eliza curtsied, causing Connie to follow suit.

Lady Victoria waved a dismissive hand at them. "Yes, of course."

As she approached him, Inspector Adams composed himself and stepped forward, offering her his hand. "We hate to disturb you at a time like this, but we're following up on the murder of your husband and wondered if you could answer a few questions. We'll try not to take up too much of your time."

Lady Victoria nodded as she held a hand across her heart before perching on the edge of the settee. "I'll try my best, although I thought someone had been arrested."

Inspector Adams smiled. "Indeed they have, but before we can formally charge him we need to be sure of the evidence. We don't want to get to court with holes in our story."

"No, I don't suppose you do. What would you like to know?"

Inspector Adams took out his notebook and held his pencil ready. "First of all, I wonder if you could tell us where you were between ten and eleven o'clock on Saturday morning?"

"That would have been after breakfast when I was with Hilda in the conservatory."

"Could you tell us what time you got there?"

Lady Victoria paused, her eyes fixed on an ornate clock on the mantelpiece. "I left almost immediately after breakfast and so it would have been about ten o'clock, give or take a few minutes."

"And you were there for the whole hour?"

"Well, yes. We were discussing the ball that evening and what we would wear."

"I see." Inspector Adams flicked through the pages of his notebook. "I ask because we have several witnesses who suggest that you weren't there for the whole hour."

For a second Eliza thought she saw confusion in Lady Victoria's blue eyes but she quickly regained her composure.

"Oh, you're right. How could I forget? I went into the garden to find David. He had some schoolwork to do and Cyril was angry that he'd gone off with Albert. I didn't know what the fuss was about because he isn't due back at school until next week, but when Cyril was in one of his moods, it was better not to argue."

"And so you went to look for him? Where did you find him?"

"I walked down the path from the conservatory and found him with Albert by the lake."

"I see." The inspector rubbed his chin. "I wonder, could you be more precise about where they were?"

Lady Victoria paused to compose herself. "Just approaching the place they ... they found Cyril." She put a hand over her eyes.

The room became silent as the inspector wrote the information in his notebook.

"Do you mind if I ask a question?" Eliza said. "Did you think it strange that Lord Albert didn't walk back to the house with you?"

Lady Victoria looked up, surprise on her face. "Not at all, why would it be? He said he was meeting someone and would follow us in."

"I don't suppose he told you who he was meeting?"

When Lady Victoria confirmed he hadn't told her, Eliza turned to the inspector. "I wonder if he was meeting his father."

Inspector Adams nodded. "It would make sense. Did you see Lord Lowton while you were by the lake, Lady Victoria?"

"Neville? No, I don't think so, should I have?"

"Not necessarily, we just want to account for everyone's whereabouts at the time and we know Lord Lowton was in the area."

"You do?" Lady Victoria's eyebrows rose.

"He was one of the first on the scene when your husband was found." Inspector Adams cut Eliza off before she could speak.

"Yes, of course." Lady Victoria seemed to relax. "Everything's such a blur for me."

"I'm sure it is, we understand." Inspector Adams put on his best smile. "May I ask one more question? Once you found your son, did you go straight back to the house?"

"We did, and I immediately took him to the library. Lord Beaufort was in there and I asked him to keep an eye on him before I went back to the conservatory."

Eliza and Inspector Adams stared at each other.

"Lord Beaufort was in the library?" Eliza said when Inspector Adams remained silent.

"Well, yes ... is there a problem with that?"

"I wouldn't like to say at the moment, but could you tell me what time this would have been?" Inspector Adams said.

"Oh, I'm not sure, maybe half past ten. Yes, it was, the clock in the hallway chimed as I was leaving the room."

"What was Lord Beaufort doing?" Eliza asked as casually as she could manage.

Lady Victoria's laugh sounded out of place on such a sombre occasion. "When we arrived, he was sitting in a wingback chair fast asleep. He wouldn't admit it, of course, and said he was thinking, but I had to point out to him that one doesn't snore when one's thinking."

Eliza turned to Inspector Adams. "It sounds like he could have been there for a while."

Before the inspector could reply, Lord David pushed open the double doors and stormed into the room.

"What's going on here?" He marched to the side of his mother. "Do you want me to get rid of them?"

Eliza was relieved when Lady Victoria shook her head. "No, they're fine. They just have a few questions about Father's death."

"Father's death?" Lord David's forehead creased. "Haven't they charged the commoner who was at the hall over the weekend?"

Eliza pulled herself up to her full height ready to reply but Inspector Adams put a hand on her shoulder.

"Not yet," he said. "Mr Bell is in custody but we haven't charged him. We don't have enough evidence against him."

"Not enough evidence! He followed Father from the house after breakfast saying he would teach him a lesson, and less than half an hour later, Uncle Neville found him with Father's dead body and the murder weapon in his hand."

Eliza's nostrils flared. "That's because he found the body, not because he was responsible for it."

"I think you'll find the evidence says otherwise." Lord David stood toe to toe with Eliza, his spindly frame towering above her.

"We have yet to discover the evidence."

"Please, Mrs Thomson, Lord David." Inspector Adams put a hand between them to push them apart. "Can we keep this civil?" Inspector Adams waited until the two of them turned away from each other, before he again flicked through his notebook. "Good, now may I go back to the inquest Lord Beaufort held? Lord David, you initially told Lord Beaufort you were in your room reading, but he would have known that was a lie. Why would that alibi suit both of you?"

Lord David looked to his mother, who pushed herself up from her seat.

"Oh, Inspector, please don't be angry with me. I told you Lord Beaufort was asleep, and he was ever so embarrassed about snoring. We said we'd pretend we hadn't seen him."

"Saying you were together in the library doesn't imply he was asleep," Eliza said. "Why lie to the one man who really knew where you were?"

"What does it matter if you know we all have alibis?" Lord David's voice filled the room.

"It matters because as things stand, an innocent man could be sent to the gallows and yet it appears that the alibis collected by Lord Beaufort are no more than a bunch of lies. From where I'm standing I would suggest you're all in it together, covering up for one another."

"What utter nonsense." Lord David no longer pretended to be polite. "Why would I protect my father's killer when I want to see him hanged?"

"Why indeed?" Connie put a hand to her mouth. "I-I'm sorry, that wasn't meant to come out."

Lord David glared at her. "I am not protecting anyone, now if you'll excuse me, I have things to do."

171

CHAPTER TWENTY

On the stroke of two o'clock the police carriage pulled up in front of the main entrance to Lowton Hall and Soams had the front door open before Eliza and Connie had alighted.

"His Lordship is waiting for you in his office," he said to Inspector Adams. "May I get you some tea?"

"No, thank you. We've just enjoyed some hospitality in the Queen's Arms in the village. A very decent public house if you don't mind me saying."

Soams nodded. "It is indeed, sir, please walk this way."

Lords Lowton and Beaufort were sitting in two wingback chairs on either side of the fireplace when they arrived. The heat from the fire and smoke from the cigars were overwhelming on such a warm day and Eliza was grateful when Soams crossed the room to open a window.

"Inspector Adams." Lord Lowton stood up to shake the inspector's hand. "I expected you to be alone."

The inspector turned to his left. "I believe you know Mrs

Thomson and Mrs Appleton. They're helping me with my enquiries, I hope you don't mind."

Lord Lowton glowered at Eliza. "I mind a great deal about this whole thing, Inspector. Beaufort here conducted an inquiry into my brother's death last Sunday, following which a man was arrested. I gave strict instructions not to involve the police and yet less than a week later, I find you here in my office. Explain yourself, man."

Inspector Adams hesitated but Eliza decided against interrupting him.

"Y-yes, of course. I'm sorry to trouble you, but before we can charge anyone with the murder, we need to make sure we have all the evidence. It's merely formalities."

"So Beaufort's investigation wasn't thorough enough for you? What else do you need to know?"

Eliza stared at the dark mahogany walls of the office as Inspector Adams fumbled with his notebook. The portraits on the walls were similar to those she had seen in Lady Victoria's drawing room and bore a clear resemblance to the current earl of Lowton. *These men must have spent hours sitting around being painted.* She was brought back to the room when the inspector began to speak.

"First of all, Lord Lowton, can you confirm where you were between ten o'clock and half past on Saturday morning?"

"You should know precisely where I was from Beaufort's report. We were in this office together, sitting in these chairs to be exact."

Inspector Adams gave a nervous cough. "Yes ... well, the thing is, we know that wasn't the case."

Eliza saw the glance that passed between their lordships before Lord Lowton rubbed at his left eye.

"Are you accusing us of not telling the truth?"

Inspector Adams visibly shrivelled under Lord Lowton's glare. "N-not at all, I just need to clear up the conflict." He flicked to another page in his notebook before returning to his original place. "For example, Lord Lowton, we know you were one of the first to reach the scene of the crime at about half past ten that morning. If you'd been in here, you wouldn't have been able to reach the lake in less than about quarter of an hour, or so I'm told."

"Perhaps I wasn't here for the whole time, but what of it? I'm not likely to murder my own brother." The twitch under Lord Lowton's eye was clearly evident.

"Even so, we do need to account for the time leading up to the death. May I ask what time you left the office and where you went?"

"If you must know, I went to the lawn near the west wing. We've had moles and they'd made a terrible mess. I couldn't tell you what time it was, but I wanted to check the traps we'd set up."

Inspector Adams nodded. "Thank you. So by my reckoning, based on the fact you were by the lake at half past ten when the body was found, I presume you were by the west wing no later than twenty past. Can anyone confirm you were there?"

"We have an estate manager, Colonel Hawkins, he was with me."

Eliza could hold her tongue no longer. "Forgive me for interrupting, but if Colonel Hawkins was with you, why did you lie about your original alibi and involve Lord Beaufort?"

"It was clearly a mistake," Lord Beaufort said. "I've been thinking about it and realised we were in here earlier than I thought. We must have misjudged the time."

All eyes turned to Lord Lowton.

"By jove, you're right, Beaufort. I had an early breakfast that day, didn't I? I clearly wasn't paying attention to the clock."

"But Lord Beaufort–" Eliza managed to hold his gaze "– we know you were in the breakfast room until about ten o'clock. That doesn't give you much time to come in here and then be in the library for half past."

"I was in here before ten o'clock, but we mustn't have sat for as long as I thought."

Connie turned to Inspector Adams, her face a picture of innocence. "If we've established that Lord Lowton was in here until about quarter past ten and then walked into the garden with the estate manager, does that leave Lord Beaufort without an alibi?"

"So it would seem." Inspector Adams studied Lord Beaufort. "Would you care to tell us what you were doing once Lord Lowton left you?"

Lord Beaufort got to his feet. "I don't like your insinuations, Inspector."

"I'm sure I wasn't making any, sir, but I trust you'll understand that we need to confirm where you were."

Lord Beaufort walked to an ashtray near the window and crushed the stub of his cigar into it.

When Lord Beaufort failed to respond, Eliza prompted him. "If you're struggling to remember, we have two witnesses who say they saw you in the library."

"Damn woman," Lord Beaufort muttered under his

breath.

"What we don't understand is why you felt the need to lie," Inspector Adams said. "If our witnesses are to be believed, you clearly had an alibi for the time of the murder."

"I told you, I got my times confused." The tone of Lord Beaufort's voice persuaded Eliza not to pursue it.

"Very well." Inspector Adams turned back to Lord Lowton. "I think we've finished here, for now at least. I wonder if we could see the part of the lawn you visited ... when you were examining the mole traps. We'll need to check the distance from the lawn to the lake. We'll also need to speak with Colonel Hawkins if he's around."

Lord Lowton's face turned red. "This is nonsense. Colonel Hawkins is a busy man, he could be on any part of the estate."

"We'll still need to speak to him though, to confirm your alibi. Does he have a house? We can visit him there at the end of the day if need be. Just to be thorough, of course."

Lord Lowton stormed to the door. "I'll get Soams to take you outside. He can point out the colonel's cottage as well. It's across the other side of the lake." He disappeared into the hallway calling for his butler.

When they returned a minute later, Lord Lowton sank into his chair by the fire while Soams waited at the door.

Inspector Adams nodded in the direction of the two gentlemen. "Thank you for your time, this has been most helpful."

They were about to leave when Eliza stopped and studied Lord Lowton. "May I ask you one last question? If you were in the gardens with Colonel Hawkins, why didn't he accompany you to the lake when Father called?"

"We had just split up and he was heading towards the wood on the western borders of the estate."

"Thank you." Eliza nodded and turned away, raising her eyebrows at Connie as Soams held the door open for them.

The walk to the lawn took the best part of five minutes and by the time they arrived, it was bathed in sunlight.

"What a beautiful lawn," Inspector Adams said.

"Indeed it is, sir, now that the moles have been eliminated."

"That must have been quite a job," Eliza said. "I remember we had moles at home once and it took Father months to be rid of them."

"Colonel Hawkins is one of the best, madam. He managed to repair the lawn in little more than a month."

Eliza tried her best to remain casual. "My goodness, he must be good. How long has he been here?"

"Since the autumn of last year."

Eliza pursed her lips. "So the moles have been gone since the end of last year? Tell me, did you see Lord Lowton out here with Colonel Hawkins on Saturday morning?"

Soams shook his head. "I'm afraid I didn't, madam. I was in and out of the marquee all day, as were most of the staff. Lady Caroline will vouch for us."

Eliza smiled. "Yes, I'm sure she will. Thank you, Soams. If you could just give us directions to Colonel Hawkins' cottage, we'll leave you to get on."

Soams pointed beyond the lake. "If you take the left-hand path down the side of the lake, you'll find a bank of cottages at the base of the hill. He occupies the first one you come to."

"Thank you so much, at least it's a lovely day for a walk."

Eliza watched Soams walk back across the garden.

"What do you make of all that then?" she said once she was sure he was out of earshot.

"I'd say we've heard a lot of things that don't add up," Connie said. "For one, why did Lord Lowton need to come and check this lawn for moles? It's immaculate."

Eliza turned in a full circle as she inspected the lawn and borders. "I don't think he was here, at least not for more than the minute or two it would take him to walk across it."

"We can check that later when we speak to Colonel Hawkins, assuming he arrives home." Inspector Adams wrote in his notebook.

Connie's eyes lit up. "Do you think Lord Lowton might make him disappear so we can't ask him any questions?"

Inspector Adams grimaced. "Let me just say, I've come across all sorts over the years and so I'll reserve judgement until later. For now, I suggest we walk down the path to the lake. If Lord Lowton really was here, I imagine this is the way he would have walked and we can estimate how long it might have taken." Inspector Adams paused. "Do you remember him being out of breath when he arrived, as if he'd been running? That would affect the time."

Eliza shook her head. "I didn't notice him being particularly breathless, only from the exertion of pulling the body from the water."

"Me neither, although I'm not sure he walked along this path," Connie said. "We were on the adjacent one and we didn't see him."

"Perhaps he was behind you and you didn't notice," Inspector Adams said.

"He could have been, but I think Connie's right. This path might be the most direct route to the lake, but I don't believe for one minute he was out here inspecting the lawn. For one, it doesn't need inspecting and secondly, why lie about it? If he really was here with the colonel, he had no need to drag Lord Beaufort into his alibi."

Inspector Adams nodded as he drew out his pocket watch. "Rather than debate it here, I suggest we walk over to the lake. I make it a quarter past three now. If we move as quickly as we can, I'll note the time we arrive. If that's the lake I can see through the trees, I doubt we'll do it in under five minutes."

Eight minutes later, and more out of breath than she would have liked, Eliza saw the expanse of lake open up before her.

"There's no possibility that Lord Lowton was on that lawn when Father called for help."

Connie was equally breathless. "So why say he was? He must have known we could check the distance."

"At least we know why the colonel wasn't with him if they separated on the lawn," Inspector Adams said.

"If they ever met at all. It's no wonder they don't want us to talk to him." Eliza put her hands on her hips as she surveyed the paths to their right. "There are several other paths, but none that go directly to the house. I've had a suspicion for a while that Lord Lowton was involved in whatever happened, and now I'm even more sure. If only we could prove it."

"Let's not get ahead of ourselves," Inspector Adams said. "I presume we're near the crime scene. Can you take me there?"

Eliza led the way and once they arrived, she immediately checked to see if the footprint was still visible.

"Here it is, Inspector." She pointed towards the edge of the lake. "This is the footprint I was telling you about. It's not the sort of impression you would make if you were just passing by for a walk."

Inspector Adams crouched down by the dried-up print. "You're right, it isn't. It looks like some force or pressure has been applied to make such a deep imprint ... in fact the mud is uneven, as if more pressure was applied to one side of the foot than the other."

Eliza bent over to take a closer look. "You're right, I hadn't noticed that. Could it have been made during a struggle?"

"It may well have been." Inspector Adams pushed himself back up. "I wish I'd taken more notice when you were talking about this; I could have got a police photographer to come and take an image. We're fortunate it's lasted so long."

He continued to stare at the print before he backed away and bent down again. "Look at this, they're faint, but there are some smaller footprints here."

"Lord Albert, would you say?" Connie asked Eliza.

She nodded. "It would make sense. He may well have stood here while he waited for his mystery visitor."

"Based on what we've heard, I would imagine he was waiting for his father." Inspector Adams studied the scene. "Although, why would they both try and hide it?"

"What if Sir Cyril caught them up to something and there was a fight?" Connie's face glowed as she spoke.

"It's an idea ... although something's not right about that." Eliza paused and bent down over the footprints again. "If Sir Cyril accidentally came upon them, how did the croquet mallet find its way here? I don't think that was an accident. I'd say someone deliberately brought that mallet intending to do some harm."

"Do you think Lady Victoria or Lord David know anything about it?" Connie asked. "They've both lied about their whereabouts that morning."

Eliza gazed at Connie as she thought. "Lord David was rather angry when we asked about it."

"Don't you think that was just the bluff of an immature young man trying to impress his mother?" Inspector Adams said. "He wants to be the man of the house now and needs to make his presence felt."

Eliza groaned. "I certainly know about immature young men but I'd say we can rule Lord David out. Unless Lady Victoria's lying, they were both back at the house by half past ten."

"She could be lying," Connie said.

"She could, but I'm inclined to believe them given they both saw Lord Beaufort in the library, something he didn't want to acknowledge, but couldn't deny."

"That doesn't mean Lord David is unaware of what went on, though," Inspector Adams said. "Do you know what the boy's relationship was like with his father?"

Eliza and Connie both shook their heads.

"I know Sir Cyril wasn't popular with the ladies of the family but I've no idea about Lord David. I could ask Caroline if you like?" Eliza said.

"Yes, why don't you?" Inspector Adams said. "I'm beginning to wonder if everyone is so glad to see the back of Sir Cyril, they're deliberately impeding our efforts to find out who murdered him."

CHAPTER TWENTY-ONE

The clock on the front of the house struck four as they walked back towards the conservatory.

Eliza stopped to listen as the third and fourth chimes rang out. "I'm not surprised we didn't hear that when we were down by the lake, even now we're closer to the house it's still quiet."

"Sir Rodney must have good hearing," Connie said. "Although I suppose he wasn't as far down the garden as we were."

"Is there any significance in the fact that he heard it, do you think?" Inspector Adams asked. "After all, we are basing a lot on Sir Rodney's claim that it sounded shortly after he saw Lord Lowton."

"And the ring for the half hour would only have comprised one strike. He must have been paying close attention." Eliza's brow furrowed. "If he misheard, or worse, is lying, it changes everything." Eliza closed her eyes before she shook her head. "No, Sir Rodney is Father's lifelong friend, he wouldn't lie about something like that." She stamped her foot. "Confound Sir Cyril. If he wasn't such a horrible man, we wouldn't be in this predicament. How are we supposed to have Father freed when no one will tell the truth?"

Inspector Adams took Eliza by the elbow. "Come along. Let's assume there's no significance in it for now. I think we're making headway."

"And it's turned four o'clock, there should be afternoon tea in the drawing room," Connie said. "If we're fortunate, we'll be the only ones there."

Inspector Adams stopped where he was. "Ah, I'd forgotten you'd be going indoors. I'll wait out here for you."

"Nonsense, you can come in as our guest, I'm sure Caroline won't mind," Eliza said.

Inspector Adams' eyebrows drew together. "I don't think Lord Lowton will be very pleased to see me."

"My guess is that he won't be there. Come along and we'll go in first to make sure the coast is clear."

The drawing room was empty when Eliza and Connie arrived, although there was a large pot of tea and a selection of sandwiches and cakes on the sideboard opposite the fire.

"Do you think Henry and Lord Albert will join us?" Connie asked.

Eliza shrugged. "I've no idea, but we haven't spoken to Lord Albert yet and so it wouldn't be a bad thing if they did. If they don't, I'll go upstairs at five o'clock and check if Henry's there."

Connie nodded. "Do you want to pour the tea and I'll go and fetch the inspector? I won't be a minute."

Connie had no sooner left than Lady Caroline walked into the room. "All on your own?"

Eliza smiled. "Caroline, good afternoon. Yes, I am for the moment, but I hope you don't mind me asking Inspector Adams to join us for a cup of tea. I would have asked you first, but when the room was empty I assumed you wouldn't mind."

"Is he still around?" Lady Caroline was dismissive as she picked up several cucumber sandwiches.

"Only for another hour or so. He's going back to London tonight, but wants a quick word with Colonel Hawkins before he goes."

"Colonel Hawkins? What on earth does he want to speak to him for? Does he think he's the killer?"

Eliza carried two cups of tea to the table in front of the fire before returning for the third. "No, not at all, but Lord Lowton said he was with him shortly before the attack on Sir Cyril, and so he needs to confirm it."

Lady Caroline raised an eyebrow but said nothing.

"Another question we had was about Lord David." Eliza ignored the sandwiches and helped herself to a piece of cake. "Was he close to his father?"

Lady Caroline shrugged. "Not especially, Cyril was very strict with him and so any interaction between them was often formal. Why?"

Eliza tried to be as casual as she could. "No reason, he just doesn't seem as upset as I might have expected. Perhaps it's the British 'stiff upper lip'."

Lady Caroline's laugh sounded false. "I'm sure it is. It wouldn't be natural if he wasn't upset, would it?"

My point exactly. Eliza took a seat close to the fire. "I'm going to visit Father again tomorrow but after that I need to go home. It's been very generous of you to let us stay, but all this has taken longer to resolve than I expected."

"So you still think your father's innocent?"

"Yes, of course, it's just proving harder than we thought to establish who the killer is."

"I did think Lord Beaufort's recommendation was a little strange at the time, but I suppose the evidence is the evidence." Lady Caroline placed a hand on Eliza's arm. "Maybe you need to accept your father's guilt."

Eliza was about to reply when the door to the drawing room opened and Connie escorted Inspector Adams in.

"Good afternoon, Inspector." Lady Caroline glided towards the door, her hand extended. "How nice of you to join us. Eliza's been telling me you haven't made much headway."

Inspector Adams turned to Eliza, who gave a subtle shake of her head. "No, that's right. We've a few more avenues to explore yet. Once I'm finished here, I'm heading back to London to see if I can make any sense of what we've learned. Sometimes it helps to sleep on these things."

"Of course. Won't you join us by the fire? It looks like Eliza has poured you some tea, but I'll bring the plate of cakes over. I'm sure you won't say no."

Eliza sipped at her tea as Lady Caroline lavished her attention on the inspector.

"You will come back and tell us what you find, won't you?" Lady Caroline said as her guests stood up to leave.

Inspector Adams bowed towards her. "I'm sure I will."

"I'm sorry we have to leave you alone but we need to catch Henry before we visit the colonel's cottage," Eliza explained. "Do you mind if we use the library?"

"No, of course not, although I'm not sure where you'll find Henry. He and Albert have been missing since breakfast."

"Well, we'd better try."

Lady Caroline nodded. "Will you join us for dinner tonight? I'll be in here from half past seven and dinner will be at eight."

"Yes, that sounds splendid, although the inspector has to go back to London so it will just be the two of us, and Henry if we can find him. We'll see you later."

Once they were clear of the drawing room, Eliza gestured to the library. "Let's check whether it's free before I look for Henry. I'm hoping he'll be waiting for me upstairs."

"Are we seeing him for any particular reason?" Inspector Adams asked once they'd established the library was empty.

Eliza put a hand to her mouth. "Of course, we didn't tell you. We spoke to Henry last night after you'd gone, Connie will tell you all about it while I go and get him."

Eliza hurried up the stairs and as soon as she rounded the corner towards her bedroom, she saw Henry sitting on the floor outside her room. He jumped to his feet as soon as he saw her.

"There you are, I was beginning to think you'd forgotten about me."

"Of course not, but we had Lady Caroline to entertain during afternoon tea. Why didn't you join us?"

Henry kicked his heels together. "I didn't feel like anything."

Eliza eyed her son; it wasn't like him to turn down food. "Never mind, come with me. We're meeting in the library."

"We?" Henry stopped, a puzzled expression across his face.

"Inspector Adams is with us, Connie's explaining to him what we asked you to find out. Come along, because we need to go out as soon as we're finished."

"I don't know enough to talk to the police!" Henry stopped, forcing Eliza to turn and face him.

"That doesn't matter. What we're doing is like a jigsaw puzzle. Each piece on its own means nothing, but when you put it all together, suddenly a picture emerges. You may just have the missing piece."

Henry resumed his walk. "I doubt it."

Inspector Adams was waiting for them as they entered the library and held out his hand to Henry as Eliza introduced them.

"Mr Thomson, very nice to meet you. Please take a seat. Now, I believe you were hoping to find out who Lord Albert was waiting for by the lake last Saturday. Did you have any success?"

Henry stared at the inspector before turning to his mother. "I'm afraid I didn't, but I did ask. I asked him directly, but he said he was sworn to secrecy."

"And he gave no hint at all of who it could be?" Inspector Adams said. "Perhaps he referred to the person as 'he' or 'she'."

Henry's eyes narrowed. "Now you mention it, he did say 'he'. I think his exact words were 'He made me promise not to tell a soul.'"

"So there was no young lady involved then?" Inspector Adams winked at Henry, who laughed.

"No, although he does have one, back in Cambridge. He said it was more than his life was worth to bring her here this weekend. He only told Lord Lowton about her on Friday night."

"Is this the girl you said was a commoner?" Eliza asked.

"That's her. She's lovely though and from a good family. He could do a lot worse."

"I suppose that's a matter of opinion when you're an earl. How did Lord Lowton take the news?"

"Not terribly well from what I could gather, but Albert wouldn't talk about it. He said he'll tell me when we get back to Cambridge."

"Well, if you find it has any bearing on this investigation, please let us know," Inspector Adams said.

"Where've you been today then?" Eliza asked.

"We had a walk around the grounds this morning and then wandered into the village for something to eat shortly after midday. There's a rather good public house there called the Queen's Arms."

Inspector Adams laughed. "We know it well, I escorted your mother and Mrs Appleton there yesterday at around the same time. Was it busy?"

"It was rather. I saw Lord Beaufort in there as well. You wouldn't expect his type..." Henry's voice trailed off when all eyes turned to look at him. "What have I said?"

"What was he doing in there?" Eliza spoke to the inspector. "Henry, can you recall *exactly* what time this would have been?"

Henry shrugged. "We probably left here at about half

past twelve and it took about half an hour to walk there. We'd got some drinks and ordered a couple of pies before I saw him come in. Around a quarter past one?"

"And was he on his own?"

"He came in on his own, but there was a man sitting alone in the corner opposite us and he joined him. It was strange though, he didn't have a drink or anything, they just spoke for several minutes before Lord Beaufort passed him an envelope. The man looked inside, nodded and Lord Beaufort left."

"Did he see you?"

Henry shook his head. "No, I don't think so. As I was saying, it was a strange place to see him and he didn't look comfortable. He kept his head down as he walked out."

"What about Lord Albert? Did he see him?"

"No, he was on a stool on the opposite side of the table to me and so he had his back to them."

Eliza was surprised when she breathed a sigh of relief.

"Can you tell us anything about the man he visited?" the inspector asked. "Had you seen him before?"

"I had, but I can't put my finger on when or where. He just seemed familiar."

"I'm going to hazard a guess here," Eliza said. "Was he a broad-shouldered man with tanned skin and a bushy moustache?"

"Y-yes." Henry stared from one to the other. "How did you know?"

"Lord Lowton conveniently came up with an alibi earlier today that contradicted everything in Lord Beaufort's original report. At the time I didn't believe him, and this adds weight to the fact he lied to us ... again. My guess is that there was money in that envelope in exchange for the false alibi."

"If that's the case, the colonel should still have the money on him." Inspector Adams turned to Henry. "We're about to visit Colonel Hawkins about the alibi. If you have time, I'd appreciate it if you'd join us and confirm that we're talking about the same man. If he is the man you saw, it could give us the evidence we need."

"I suppose so, if you think I could help."

"While we're heading that way, could we go via the boot room and pick up one of Lord Lowton's shoes?" Eliza said. "I'm sure he made the footprint at the side of the lake and the imprint of the sole is distinctive enough that we should be able to find it."

Inspector Adams scratched his head. "I'm not sure about that, we can't just go taking shoes. What if he misses it?"

"We won't be long, I'll take it back before dinner."

"We can't all go to the boot room." Connie fidgeted with her fingers. "It's so close to the kitchen, someone might see us."

"All right," Eliza said. "Let me go by myself. I had another good look at the footprint the other day and I'm sure there was a pair of boots that matched. I'll meet you on the west lawn in quarter of an hour."

CHAPTER TWENTY-TWO

Eliza hurried upstairs, before moving with equal speed down to the boot room. Fifteen minutes later, with a bulging blanket tucked under her arm, she dashed across the lawn to the group waiting for her.

She pointed to her makeshift package. "I've got the shoe, but you'll never guess what else I found? The croquet mallet!"

"Oh, well done." Connie clapped her hands under her chin.

"Are you sure it's the same one?" Inspector Adams asked.

"Yes, certain. Someone had pushed it into a corner of the boot room with a selection of brushes, probably to disguise it, but it's got some telltale marks on it. I didn't want to disturb the evidence and so I left it where it was for now. I'll show it to you on the way back."

Inspector Adams nodded. "Good idea."

"I hope nobody saw you," Connie said.

"No, I'm sure they didn't, most of the staff are busy."

"Well, I hope they're still busy when we get back."

Eliza grinned. "I'll think of something to say if anyone sees me. I know, I'll make sure I get mud on my shoes and tell them they need cleaning. Don't let me forget. Come on, shall we go?"

Once they reached the bank of rhododendron bushes, Eliza unwrapped the shoe but stopped dead when she reached the side of the lake.

"It's gone!" She stared at Inspector Adams, her left forefinger pointing at the spot. "It's as if someone's deliberately destroyed it."

Inspector Adams bent down to inspect the disturbed soil. "It looks like someone dragged their heel over the spot several times, the grooves are deep."

"Is there nothing to salvage?"

Inspector Adams shook his head. "No, they did a good job."

"Lord Beaufort could have asked the man in the public house to do it," Henry said.

Eliza couldn't take her eyes from the spot. "I don't know, perhaps he did, but we were only here a couple of hours ago and the print was in perfect condition." Eliza's brow furrowed before she turned to the inspector. "Do you think someone followed us down here earlier?"

"Nobody knew we were coming. We only decided when we were talking to Soams."

"Soams!" Eliza said. "He could have gone back to the office to tell His Lordship what we were doing."

"But he's such a nice man..." Connie said.

"Who works for Lord Lowton and, I imagine, is very loyal," Eliza added.

"But if somebody followed us, how did we not see them?"

Eliza finally dragged her eyes from the disturbed earth and examined the bushes. "Perhaps it was the same way nobody saw Lords Lowton and Albert after Sir Cyril had been murdered."

"A hiding place you mean?"

"That's exactly what I mean." Eliza turned a full circle as she inspected each angle for a possible hideout. "Let's split up. Connie, you and I should take a closer look at the bushes; Inspector Adams, can you and Henry examine the paths to either side?"

They worked in silence for several minutes until there was a shout from Henry. "Over here." He stood back and pointed towards the lake from the right-hand path.

"There's nothing there," Eliza said when she joined him.

"Wait a minute." Inspector Adams stepped forward into the shrubbery that lined the path. "There's a trench."

The group moved forward to see a split in the ground.

"I'd say it was made by the tree roots, but it's grown so deep it would be easy enough for someone to hide themselves if they wanted to."

As if to prove the point, Henry jumped into the ditch.

"Oh my goodness." Eliza's mouth fell open as she turned to Connie. "Come with me. We're going back to the footprint. Henry, I want you to tell me if you can hear us talking."

Eliza hadn't realised she could still move so fast, but within a minute she was back beside the lake. "Right, Henry, can you hear us?"

"I'm not very far from you." Henry stuck his head up from the trench much closer than expected, causing Eliza and Connie to jump.

"How did you get there?"

"The trench leads all the way to the water, you just can't see it because there's an overhang."

"Is it wet in there then?"

"No, it's not." A frown crossed Henry's face before he disappeared only to reappear moments later. "The end's blocked up."

"I wonder why." Eliza mused about the finding while Henry found a place to haul himself out of the trench.

"It didn't take you long to get out of the ditch and get back here," Eliza said. "And your trousers and shoes aren't muddy either."

"It's a good job it's not been raining, it'd be messy if it had."

Connie moved as close to the edge of the ditch as she dared and peered over. "Are there any footprints down there? We know the ground was softer on Saturday."

Henry returned to the ditch and slowly walked the length of it. "There are a couple here." He stopped just before the place he had spoken to Eliza. "Pass me that boot down and I'll see if they match."

Inspector Adams didn't wait for Henry's verdict before hurrying to the opening and climbing into the ditch.

"It looks like this matches some of the prints down here," Henry said.

"Good gracious, so it does." Inspector Adams was breathless as he took the boot from Henry. "There are several sets and they're all faint and rather scuffed, but there's enough to say that whoever was wearing this boot has been in this ditch."

"So it must have been Lord Lowton," Connie said.

"Not necessarily. We can't assume this is his shoe, or that he was wearing it, but at least we've got something to work with." Inspector Adams stood up and patted Henry on the back. "Well done, Mr Thomson. I don't think we'd have found this without you."

Henry beamed at his mother but her focus remained on the trench.

"They've been playing games with us all along, haven't they? Well, they picked the wrong person..."

"Mrs Thomson, may I have your attention?" Inspector Adams tucked away his pocket watch. "We need to move. Colonel Hawkins should be home shortly and I still need to get back to London. Henry, bring the shoe with you. We can't afford to lose it."

Ten minutes later, as the four of them walked along the left-hand side of the lake, the row of terraced cottages came into view at the bottom of a gentle slope.

"Soams said it was the first cottage," Eliza said. "It doesn't look like anyone's at home. All the others have their lights on."

Inspector Adams chuckled. "That means nothing. He's a man living on his own, who may be perfectly happy sitting by the light of the fire. Come on, let's go and knock."

Five minutes later, they were still on the footpath.

"Soams didn't tell us there was no path down this hill, nor that the hill was so steep," Eliza said. "Do you think he did that on purpose?"

"I would say so," Connie said. "If you ask me, this just proves they don't want us to speak to the colonel."

"Come this way." Henry pointed towards a well-trodden

path hidden amongst the bushes. "I'm sure it leads down to the road in front of the cottages."

Eliza looked down at her skirt before shaking her head at Connie. "These skirts will be more of a hindrance than usual."

"Well, we can't do much about them," Connie said. "Come on, let's give it a try."

Henry led the way but halfway down Eliza called for him to wait as her hem once again snagged on some overgrown brambles. She had stopped to inspect the damage when a movement off to the left caught her eye. "What was that?"

Connie had stopped to inspect her own skirt but straightened up as she noticed the home of Lady Victoria. "That's Lowton Farm Cottage, isn't it?"

"It most certainly is but what's Colonel Hawkins doing coming out of the front door?"

Connie gazed down the road. "I suppose they're neighbours. I imagine he was checking she was all right."

"That's the man from the pub," Henry said as he scurried back to join them. "I remember now where I saw him. He was at the ball with Lady Victoria on Friday. You don't think they're having an affair, do you?"

"Henry Thomson, wash your mouth out this minute. Lady Victoria is only recently widowed."

Henry stared at his feet. "Sorry."

Inspector Adams grinned at Henry as he climbed back up the hill to join them. "You're sure that's the man you saw?"

"Positive. He even has on the same tweed suit."

"Excellent, well done, young man. You may well have

provided us with another vital piece of information. You can go back to the house now. We'll take it from here."

"Go back?"

Eliza eyed her son. "I thought you said we should leave it all to the police."

Henry kicked at a bramble on the edge of the path. "Well, if the inspector needs help, who am I to refuse?"

"As long as it won't make you an embarrassment." The corners of Eliza's mouth curled up as she spoke.

"No, it won't." Henry grinned back at her. "I'm sorry for what I said, I was being an idiot."

"I suppose you're forgiven, this once."

Inspector Adams checked his pocket watch again. "Come along, we haven't got time for this."

"I'm sorry, Inspector, I'm coming," Eliza said. "You'd better wait here, Henry. It will be bad enough three of us calling on Colonel Hawkins, let alone four."

Henry's shoulders slumped. "Why do I miss out?"

"Because you're only a beginner. Just stay here and keep your eyes open. You never know what you might see."

With Henry sitting forlornly on an outcrop of rock, Eliza checked he still had the shoe, before she planted a kiss on his cheek. "We won't be long."

Eliza, Connie and the inspector edged a little further down the hill and watched as the colonel let himself into the house. Once the door was closed behind him, they moved from the shelter of the bushes.

"Let me do the talking," the inspector said to Eliza. "We don't want to frighten him."

The colonel's front door opened within seconds of the inspector rapping his knuckles on it.

"Good evening, sir. I'm Inspector Adams from New Scotland Yard investigating the murder of Sir Cyril Lowton last Saturday. Would you mind if we come in?"

The colonel looked from the inspector to the ladies and back again before he stepped back to hold the door open for them.

"What can I do for you?" Colonel Hawkins asked.

"Nothing for you to worry about, sir, we'd just like to confirm your whereabouts between ten and eleven o'clock last Saturday morning."

The colonel sucked air through his teeth. "Last Saturday, now, that was the day of the ball if I'm not mistaken. Let me think. I was around the front of the house for most of the day, making sure the gardens were at their best before the guests arrived."

"Would that have included the hour between ten and eleven?"

"No!"

Eliza and Connie jumped at the colonel's raised voice.

"I met with His Lordship around then. He wanted me to put more of those mole traps down. No idea why, the blighters have been gone for months."

Inspector Adams paused. "Would they be for the moles you'd eliminated on the west lawn?"

"Exactly! They'd been gone for months; why he suddenly wanted me to put traps back, I've no idea. I suppose he didn't want any molehills damaging the lawns."

"Do you still have traps set up?"

The colonel gave a vigorous shake of his head. "Not any more, I got rid of them the following morning. Unsightly things."

"And so on the Saturday, when you'd finished on the west lawn, you returned to the front of the house?"

"I did, left His Lordship and spent the rest of the day out there."

"Can you be more precise about the time you were with Lord Lowton?" Eliza said, as Inspector Adams returned to his notebook.

"No idea." The colonel took a seat by the fireplace before a large black Labrador rested its head on his knee. "My hearing's not what it used to be. A shell, you know. It went off no more than twenty feet in front of me. Unless I'm standing next to a clock, I can't hear the blessed thing chiming and I can't be checking my pocket watch every five minutes." He bashed the palm of his hand against his left ear. "It forced me from the army, the damn thing."

"So, you were fortunate to get a job here, with a house as well?"

"You could say that." The colonel smiled. "His Lordship was in charge of my regiment and when he found out I'd been an estate manager before I signed up for the army, he offered me the job. Splendid chap he is."

"Did you know Sir Cyril as well?"

The joviality dropped from the colonel's face. "A nasty piece of work he was. You shouldn't speak ill of the dead, but there's not many around here sorry to see the back of him. Even the dog didn't like him. I can't take him near their cottage." He rubbed the top of the dog's head.

"Really?" Inspector Adams raised an eyebrow and waited for the colonel to continue.

"He always hated the fact his brother inherited the estate

rather than him and he made everyone's life a misery because of it. He found fault in everything and everyone."

"But you enjoy Lady Victoria's company?" Eliza said.

The colonel froze, only his eyes moving from Eliza and Connie back to the inspector. "Yes, of course, she's a very nice lady. Always considerate."

"We saw you leaving her cottage as we were making our way here. Do you keep an eye out for her?"

The colonel's face reddened. "She's in that house on her own with very few visitors. I like to call in to check she's safe."

"That's very kind of you, I'm sure," Inspector Adams said. "Mrs Thomson and Mrs Appleton said you escorted her to the ball on Saturday as well. Did you know at that stage Sir Cyril was dead?"

"Good heavens, no. For one, I wouldn't have let them put the body in the folly like they did. It made a terrible mess. I don't know what His Lordship was thinking."

"So when did you find out?" Eliza asked.

"Hmm. Sometime the following day. I was helping to tidy up around the marquee and saw Lord Beaufort. He told me."

"You're rather friendly with Lord Beaufort, I believe." Inspector Adams raised an eyebrow. "Didn't you have a drink with him in the Queen's Arms earlier today?"

This time not even the colonel's eyes moved as he stared at the inspector.

"How did you know that?" he managed, eventually.

"Someone from the hall saw you. He said Lord Beaufort passed you an envelope. Would you mind if we saw what was inside?"

Colonel Hawkins was on his feet faster than Eliza believed was possible, the dog barking as his peace was disturbed.

"Who's been talking about me? That was a private conversation ... about a private matter ... held in private. I know my rights, I don't need to tell you anything but I will tell you this, I didn't kill him."

Inspector Adams held up his hands. "I'm sorry, calm down, I wasn't implying that you had. I realise you would have been busy on Saturday. It just seems an unlikely friendship, that's all."

The colonel let out a low, grumbling sound. "Well, we'll say no more about it then." He walked over to the door and held it open. "Good evening, Inspector."

CHAPTER TWENTY-THREE

Eliza found Henry waiting for them where she had left him, but rather than walking down the hill to join them, he stayed where he was and beckoned them towards him.

"What is it?" Eliza asked.

"Lord Lowton's just gone into the cottage." He nodded towards Lady Victoria's house.

Eliza stared at the house, willing the walls to reveal what was going on inside. "How long's he been in there?"

"Five, maybe ten minutes. He arrived not long after you'd gone to speak to the colonel." Henry didn't take his eyes off the house. "The strange thing is, he came in his carriage, but got dropped off just before the colonel's cottage. I panicked at first because I thought he might find you there, but he dismissed the driver and once he was alone, he turned and walked back to Lady Victoria's."

"Well, she's certainly popular," Connie said.

"But why would he keep his visit secret? It wouldn't be

unusual for him to call and check up on her." Eliza tapped her fingers on her lips as she thought.

"Like the colonel did?" Connie said.

"Exactly. It clearly isn't as straightforward as all that."

"He may have designs on her as well." Henry grinned as Eliza opened her mouth to chastise him.

"Will you stop that? What's got into you since you went up to Cambridge?" Eliza's cheeks turned a deep shade of pink.

Inspector Adams smirked at Henry before he checked his watch for the umpteenth time. "If it's all the same to you, I have to go. There's a train at half past six and I need to be on it."

"Shall we stay and keep an eye on the cottage?" Henry asked.

"You could, but I wouldn't stay too long. Lord Lowton could be here to escort her to dinner, by which time it will be almost dark."

"He could be, but if that's the case, why did he send the carriage away?" Eliza said. "You'd expect it to wait."

"Somehow I can't see her walking," Connie said.

"No, quite. It's just so infuriating. It wouldn't surprise me if he's the man we're after, but he's got enough power and money to get people to say and do what he wants." Eliza turned to Inspector Adams. "What do we do now? And when will you come back? I told Caroline we'd be leaving tomorrow once I've seen Father again."

"Tomorrow?" The inspector grimaced. "I had hoped you'd be here all week."

"I will be," Henry said.

The inspector nodded, but turned back to Eliza. "Can you delay your departure at least until the afternoon? If Lord Lowton's got anything to do with it, I'm out of my depth and need to speak to the chief constable about what to do next. If I'm fortunate, he'll see me first thing in the morning, but I'll need to take him through all the evidence, and who knows what he'll say? I can send you a telegram to let you know what's happening."

Eliza nodded. "That shouldn't be a problem. I'm going to the police station in the morning anyway and Caroline will expect us to stay for luncheon. I hope they've not moved Father yet."

Inspector Adams gave a sympathetic smile. "He might prefer it if they did. That cell in the police station isn't ideal."

"There isn't a cell in the world that's ideal for an innocent man."

With the inspector gone, Eliza and Connie perched on the edge of a rock next to Henry.

"The inspector's right, we can't stay here too long, can we?" Connie said.

"Do we have to go back for dinner though?" Henry said. "It's so dull and we need to talk about what we've learned."

Eliza covered her mouth to hide a grin. "We can hardly avoid it when we're the only visitors. Come on, we'd better go, otherwise we'll be late and I do need to put this shoe back." She put her hand to her mouth. "I didn't show the inspector the croquet mallet. Let's hope it's still there."

Once they reached the top of the bank leading back to the lake, Eliza stopped to assess the damage to her skirt.

"It looks like I won't be wearing this again. It's a good job we're leaving tomorrow."

Connie groaned when she saw her own skirt. "You're

right, look at me. At least your skirt's navy, not pale blue like mine."

Eliza laughed. "On the positive side, if anyone catches me in the boot room I won't have to make any excuses about needing my shoes cleaned, look at the state of them."

The light was growing dim as they arrived back at the house and Eliza led the way to the boot room. "Quick, down here."

The three of them hurried down the steps in silence before Eliza put her head around the door to check they were alone.

"In you get." She closed the door behind them and with the shoe replaced she walked to the corner of the room where the croquet mallet had been hidden.

"Blimey, how did you find that?" Henry said.

Eliza shrugged. "Just a bit of snooping, and look here, you can tell it's the murder weapon by the specks of blood."

"Should we leave it where it is or take it with us?" Connie asked.

Eliza sighed. "That's a good question and one I've not got an answer to. If we leave it here, someone may take it, but if we take it, it's only our word it was ever here."

"Perhaps we should leave it then," Henry said. "If it goes missing again, it suggests that someone is still following us ... and it will look very suspicious."

Eliza nodded. "You're right. Come on, we'd better go and get changed. We're already late."

By the time Eliza was ready for dinner, it was almost ten minutes to eight.

"Caroline will wonder where we are," she said as she

joined Connie in their sitting room. "I just hope I can look Lord Lowton in the eye after everything we've learned."

"I know," Connie said. "It's so frustrating having to wait for Inspector Adams to get back to us. It's times like this I'm glad you do all the talking."

"You mean sometimes you don't...?" Eliza grinned at her friend as the door opened and Henry stuck his head around it.

"Are you ready?"

"Yes, I think so." Eliza ran a hand down her emerald green skirt. "Let's go and see what awaits us."

The three of them made their way to the drawing room and Eliza was surprised to find Lady Caroline sitting on her own.

"Where is everyone?" she asked as she helped herself to a glass of sherry.

"You tell me." Lady Caroline said. "Since you brought Inspector Adams here, everyone's been behaving very bizarrely. I've barely seen Neville today, and as for Albert, I don't even know where he is, let alone whether he's joining us for dinner. Why couldn't you leave well alone?"

Eliza stood with her mouth open as she gawked at her friend.

"Because she doesn't want Grandfather being hanged for a crime he didn't commit," Henry said.

"Yes, exactly," Eliza said. "You shouldn't want Father hanged either."

"I don't. You should know me, I don't want anyone hanged, it's just so infuriating that Cyril is being as much a nuisance dead as he was when he was alive. You should have listened to Neville. He said we should never have brought the police into this."

"Caroline, you can't just cover up a murder."

"Why not? Especially when it's deserved. Whoever did this, did everyone a favour. They should be rewarded not punished."

Eliza put her sherry back on the sideboard and walked towards the fire where Lady Caroline sat. "I can't believe I'm hearing this."

"Oh, Eliza, don't be so naïve. Do you know nothing about how society works?"

"I know enough to know it's rotten."

Lady Caroline sighed as she flicked at her nails. "Lord Beaufort had his inquiry and found your father guilty. I was as shocked as you by the verdict but you need to accept it and let us get on with our lives."

"Is that what all these lies are about?" Eliza stood with her hands on her hips. "You don't want your little world spoiled by the inconvenient death of someone you didn't care for? What about our lives? We've found out that half the people interviewed by Lord Beaufort lied to him. How could he have come to the right conclusion if he wasn't told the truth?"

"He's a highly respected man, I'm sure he knew what he was doing." As the gong sounded for dinner, Lady Caroline finished her sherry and stood up. "We need to go through. Cook has tried a new venison dish for us and I'll be annoyed if Neville misses it."

CHAPTER TWENTY-FOUR

The following morning as the village clock struck ten, Lord Lowton's carriage carrying Eliza, Connie and Henry pulled up outside the police station.

Eliza eyed the small red-brick building with its ornate gable while she waited for Connie and Henry to alight. "I hope they've not taken him to London without telling me."

"It can't be much fun staying in a place like this." Henry strolled to the door before holding it open.

"I know, but I would like to see him before they move him. Let's go in, shall we?" Eliza straightened her back as she walked to the desk. "Good morning, Sergeant. Would it be possible to speak to Mr Bell, please?"

"It's Mr Bell's daughter, isn't it?" The sergeant took a ring of keys from a hook on the wall. "It's a good job you're here this morning. He's being moved this afternoon on the orders of the chief constable."

"The chief constable? Why has the order come from him?"

The sergeant shrugged. "Don't ask me, I just follow me

orders. I wondered if that was why you were here, but obviously not. Follow me."

Mr Bell jumped to his feet as soon as he saw them. "You're here. And Henry, too. Come on in." He glanced around the tiny cell. "I'm sorry I can't offer you more suitable surroundings."

"Stop fussing." Eliza smiled as she planted a kiss on his cheek. "How've you been since yesterday?"

Mr Bell's shoulders drooped. "Not good if I'm being honest, but I'd rather not talk about that."

"Well, before we go any further, here. I've brought you a couple of hard-boiled eggs and some bread and butter. Shall I ask the sergeant to make you a cup of tea?"

Mr Bell's face brightened. "You can try if you like, but he's not very responsive. I need to keep reminding him."

Eliza peered through the small window in the door but when she couldn't see the sergeant she sat down again. "I'll call him later. You eat that while we tell you what we've discovered."

"Have you worked out who did it?"

Despite knowing they were alone, Eliza lowered her voice. "We think so, but it could be tricky proving it."

Mr Bell's eyes glistened. "Who?"

"Lord Lowton."

"No!"

"Yes!" Connie's eyes sparkled as she spoke.

"The thing is, we think the whole family's involved," Eliza said. "They all seem to know things they're not telling us and most of them lied about their alibis."

"And that fool Beaufort didn't notice?"

Eliza checked behind her again. "We think he's involved too."

Mr Bell let out a long, low whistle. "That's quite an accusation but why would Lord Lowton kill his own brother? And why would everyone protect him?"

Eliza's brow furrowed. "That's something we're still not sure about, but it seems that everyone had a reason to dislike Sir Cyril. I can't say I've seen anyone upset about his death, except possibly Lady Victoria for the few minutes when she was playing the role of the grieving widow."

"It hasn't stopped her social life though," Connie said.

"Don't tell me, I'll wager there's been no shortage of admirers asking after her."

"You noticed that too?" Henry grinned at his grandfather. "Mother thought I was being vulgar."

"That's because she's your mother." A sparkle returned to Mr Bell's eyes.

"All right," Eliza said. "She may be attractive but that's no reason to suspect she'd have a gentlemen friend so soon after Sir Cyril's death."

"I'll tell you this," Mr Bell said. "She's too attractive and wealthy to have put up with Sir Cyril without there being something in it for her."

Eliza stared at her father. "What do you mean? You're not suggesting she had a male companion even before Sir Cyril died."

"I told you she did." Henry couldn't hide his delight. "I knew that estate manager was doing more than a routine call."

"An estate manager?" Mr Bell gaped at his grandson.

"Colonel Hawkins, ex-army. Mother wouldn't believe me when I suggested it."

"That's enough," Eliza said before turning to Mr Bell. "You'll have seen him. He was the broad-shouldered man with the tanned skin and bushy moustache who was with her at the ball."

"I remember him. He certainly looked like more than a hired hand. Have they been seen together since?"

Henry winked at his grandfather. "We saw him coming out of her cottage last night with a rather broad grin on his face."

Mr Bell paused. "So it sounds serious. I wonder if Sir Cyril knew about it."

"Surely he wouldn't have tolerated it if he did?" Eliza said.

"That's the thing," Mr Bell said. "Their type puts up with a lot, as long as they keep it amongst themselves, but if she'd taken a shine to the hired hand, well, that would be different. Sir Cyril would have hated it, but he wouldn't have been able to do much about it. She had the higher status and probably more money from her family than he did from his. All he could do was wait until her attention turned back to someone more suitable."

"Really?" Eliza's eyes were wide.

"That must have been why Lord Lowton paid her a visit last night." Henry lowered his voice as he spoke to his grandfather. "He even missed dinner. Lady Caroline wasn't happy!"

"Henry, enough of that. You know nothing of what happened last night."

Mr Bell took Eliza's hand. "Let him have his bit of fun,

although it does have a serious side. Lord Lowton could have been up to anything. You know, for years I envied Rodney because his daughter had married an earl while you ... well, you know, but after this weekend, I realise I've been wrong. Unless you're born an aristocrat, you'll never be one, however hard you try. Caroline's never been accepted and look what she's had to put up with. I suspect you've had a better life."

"They're all at it though," Henry said. "Albert's fallen for a girl at Cambridge who he wants to marry. He told his father on Friday."

Mr Bell's hazel eyes pierced Henry. "How did Lord Lowton take that news?"

"Not well from what I heard. Albert said he'd tell me the whole story when we're back at Cambridge."

Mr Bell stood up to pace the cell, but when his passage was restricted by so many legs he leaned against the wall. "I wonder if Lord Lowton mentioned it to Sir Cyril. I remember Rodney telling me how hostile he had been to Caroline joining the family. He believed that members of the upper classes should only associate with their own type. If Lady Victoria was fraternising with a hired hand, and he found out his nephew wanted to marry a commoner, I imagine he would have been furious."

"If he was that angry, wouldn't it have been him who wanted to kill someone, rather than him being the victim?" Eliza said.

"Yes, I suppose you're right."

Henry's forehead creased. "If he'd been in a fight with someone, that might be different."

"Can you really see Lord Lowton brawling with his brother?" Eliza asked.

"It might not have been His Lordship, it could have been the colonel. Perhaps Sir Cyril wanted to put an end to his liaison with Lady Victoria but the colonel was too strong for him."

Mr Bell nodded at his grandson. "You're right, that's much more likely."

"Do you really think so?" Eliza looked from one to the other. "I hadn't even considered that."

"It's a suggestion, nothing more," Mr Bell said.

"That wouldn't explain the envelope of money though," Connie said. "Why would Lord Beaufort pay the colonel for that?"

"It could have been to keep him quiet, or..." Henry's eyes brightened as he sat up straight. "...or maybe that was the plan. What if it wasn't Sir Cyril who picked the fight but the colonel? What if he was acting under orders from Lord Lowton to get rid of his brother? He's ex-army, don't forget, he'd know what he was doing."

"Good grief." Eliza stared at her father and son. "That puts a whole new complexion on things. Do you think Lord Lowton paid the colonel to kill Sir Cyril?"

"No, we're not saying that, or at least I'm not," Mr Bell said. "What's this money you're talking about? It's the first I've heard of it."

"Yes, of course, we haven't got to that." Eliza took a deep breath. "It all started with Lord Lowton lying about his alibi. When we pointed out that he couldn't have been in his office at the time he said he was, he changed it to say he had been in the garden with Colonel Hawkins."

"But we think he lied about that alibi too," Henry said. "I saw Lord Beaufort in a public house giving an envelope of money to the colonel. We thought it was so the colonel would give Lord Lowton an alibi, but what if it's more than that?"

"You are getting a bit carried away, we don't know he gave him any money," Eliza said.

"Well, what else would you put in an envelope like that?"

"It could have been anything and, unfortunately, speculation won't win in court. When we called on Colonel Hawkins last night, he wouldn't show us what was in the envelope and so we can't prove anything."

"Well, what about the footprint then ... and the trench?" Henry asked.

Mr Bell sat back down alongside Henry. "Is this the footprint by the lake?"

"It was, but we took one of Lord Lowton's boots to check it for size and when we got there, someone had destroyed it!"

"Are you sure it wasn't damaged by accident?"

Eliza shook her head. "No, it was deliberate. The thing is, we found a trench near the spot Sir Cyril was murdered and we suspect someone's been watching us while we've examined the crime scene. We also think Lord Lowton was hiding in the ditch when you found the body. That was how he got to the scene so quickly."

"If that was the case he'd know full well I didn't kill him."

"Exactly, so why else would he let everyone think it was you who killed Sir Cyril, unless he wants you to take the blame for something *he* did?"

A pained expression crossed Mr Bell's face. "Would he really do that? Knowingly send me to the gallows for a crime he committed?"

Eliza sighed. "That's what we can't prove. We just

haven't got enough evidence to link him to the murder ... and the evidence we do have, someone's destroying."

"We think that was how he knew where the mallet was when Eliza hid it in the bushes," Connie said.

Mr Bell's brow creased. "You think Lord Lowton was lurking in the ditch and watched you hide the mallet? Surely a man of his distinction wouldn't do such a thing? I can understand him hiding if he'd just murdered Sir Cyril, but he wouldn't be waiting around to watch you."

"Maybe that's what Colonel Hawkins was being paid for. To spy on us," Connie said.

Eliza considered the idea. "That's a possibility, although I doubt he knew about the murder so soon. I suppose it could have been Lord Albert; he wasn't with us when I hid the mallet."

"He was on his way back to us if I remember rightly," Connie said. "You hid the mallet when you heard him approaching."

"I did."

"Did you ever find the mallet?" Mr Bell asked.

"We did, but only yesterday when I went to get one of Lord Lowton's shoes from the boot room. Someone had hidden it in a corner behind a shoe rack. I told Inspector Adams about it, but he left without seeing it." Eliza shook her head. "That was Lord Lowton's fault too for paying Lady Victoria a visit. We were too busy waiting for him to come out of the house and the inspector had to leave. I just hope it's still there when he gets back."

"Eliza, you need to be careful." Mr Bell's face was stern. "Do you think anyone followed you last night?"

Eliza put her hands to her face. "I don't know, I don't

think so, but it's just so infuriating. I'm still sure Lord Lowton's the man we want, either directly or indirectly. Why can't we just get him to admit it?"

Mr Bell took his daughter's hands. "I know you're trying your best but you're asking the impossible. Men like him, especially with Lord Beaufort at his side, don't answer to people like us."

"But it's so unfair…"

"All's not lost yet. You know I'm being taken to London later? They say they're going to charge me, but I've been in touch with my solicitor and he's meeting me once I get there. He's been doing some digging of his own."

Eliza wiped a tear from her left eye. "Well, I hope he has more success than me. I've not given up yet but it's hard when he's got so much money and power. We're going back to Lowton Hall now but once we've had luncheon, we're going home. I'll do everything I can to get you released, but you'll need to be patient with me."

CHAPTER TWENTY-FIVE

By the time they returned to Lowton Hall, Eliza had composed herself but she still took a deep breath as the carriage pulled up outside the front door.

"I need to get away from this place. It was naïve to think I could stay here while we were looking for the real murderer. As soon as we've had luncheon, I'll ask Soams if the driver can take us to the train station."

Connie sighed and placed a hand on Eliza's arm. "Don't be so down. I'm sure you're on the verge of finding out what happened."

"I know what happened." Eliza paused for another breath. "I just can't prove it."

"Well, perhaps Inspector Adams has had some joy this morning. There may be a telegram waiting for us."

With his usual impeccable timing Soams had the door open for them by the time they climbed down from the carriage.

"Thank you, Soams. Has there been a telegram for us this morning?" Eliza made her voice as cheerful as she could.

"No, madam, I'm afraid not. Luncheon's about to be served and so would you care to go through to the dining room? If a telegram arrives, I'll have it brought through. Let me take your coats."

"He seemed keen to get us into luncheon," Eliza said.

"Perhaps he could tell you were trying to delay it ... or maybe it's his afternoon off and he wants to get away."

A smile flickered across Eliza's lips. "That's more like it. Come on, let's see what awaits us."

They entered the dining room to find Lord Lowton sitting to the right, at the head of the table, with Lord Beaufort on his right-hand side and Lady Caroline sitting opposite him to their left.

"Good afternoon." Eliza and Connie spoke together as they took their seats to the left of Lord Lowton. Henry mumbled something as he scurried to the seat next to Lord Beaufort.

"How's your father?" Lady Caroline asked.

"He's fine, thank you. Looking forward to getting out."

Lord Lowton exchanged a glance with Lord Beaufort.

"We'd heard he was being transferred to London," Lord Lowton said.

"Yes, they mentioned that, but hopefully he'll be out soon enough." Eliza sat back in her chair as a footman placed a bowl of soup in front of her. "We've gathered quite a lot of evidence in the last few days which may help his case."

Lord Beaufort smirked at Lord Lowton. "I doubt it."

"Why?" Eliza's eyes flicked between the two men.

"Because Beaufort here has submitted the details of his inquiry, along with a recommendation to charge Mr Bell, to

New Scotland Yard. His evidence will outweigh anything you can come up with."

"You don't know that." Eliza glared at Lord Lowton. "Lord Beaufort's interviews were far too basic to carry any weight in court. He didn't even provide alibis for half the men questioned ... unless he's changed them." Eliza noticed the twitch under Lord Lowton's eye and turned her attention to the soup.

"Are you doubting Beaufort's professional abilities? He interviewed everyone who was here and came up with a well-reasoned and plausible conclusion."

Eliza rested her spoon on the bowl. "I agree he interviewed everyone here, except for Lady Victoria and her children, of course, but I think his conclusions are far from robust."

"Now look here, madam..." Lord Beaufort spluttered into his soup.

"No, I won't, this charade has gone on for long enough. From what we've seen, I would say that everyone who stayed here last weekend knows who murdered Sir Cyril and yet to protect yourselves, you're prepared to let an innocent man go to his death."

Lord Lowton rubbed at his eye. "You can't prove he's innocent. He was at the scene of the crime with the murder weapon in his hand when we caught him."

"And do you know that because you were in the ditch by the lake when he happened upon the body."

"Ditch? What are you talking about? I saw him when I arrived at the lake."

"Rather too quickly for a man who said he'd been on the lawn near the house. I think you saw the whole thing."

"What utter nonsense. The man was caught red-handed."

"If he was the murderer, why would he shout for help almost immediately? It would make more sense for him to disappear quietly before anyone found the body ... like you did."

"I beg your pardon!" Lord Lowton threw his napkin onto the table but Eliza refused to back down.

"We know you were near the scene of the crime, closer than you care to admit judging by your alibi, and yet you didn't raise the alarm. Why wouldn't you call for help if you found your brother yourself?"

"Because I didn't find his body."

Eliza pursed her lips and took a deep breath. "Is that because when you found him he was very much alive?"

The room fell silent and Eliza's heart skipped a beat as Lord Lowton glowered down at her.

"Get out of my house. I will not be accused of murdering my own brother by some ... some ... woman!"

"Believe me, I'm leaving as soon as I can, but there are several questions I want answering first. Connie, do you have the cufflink?"

Connie reached into her handbag before holding it up. "You mean this one?"

"Yes, that's the one," Eliza said as she took it from her.

"Where did you get that?" Lord Lowton grabbed for it across the table, but Eliza snatched her hand away. "I'll report you to the police for theft."

Eliza glared at him. "We found it by the lake ... close to a distinctive footprint that was in the mud close to the water's edge."

"And you're suggesting that because you found my cufflink and footprint on the ground near *my* lake, it proves I'm a murderer. Of course my footprint was there, I pulled my brother from the water. I must have dropped the cufflink in the turmoil."

"I remember you were in the process of hauling Sir Cyril from the water when Mrs Appleton and I arrived, but as I remember, you didn't go near the edge of the lake, you were on the footpath pulling his shoulders."

"Well, either it was made at a different time or it's not my footprint."

"There's not much doubt it's yours. I found the pair of boots that in all probability made the print."

A frown crossed Lord Lowton's face. "How could you? All my boots are in the boot room..." His mouth dropped open. "Have you been in there? How dare you?"

"I dared because I will not stand by while the police charge my father for a murder he didn't commit, while you don't even have an acceptable alibi."

"Not all my shoes are unique, any other man could have made that footprint."

"That's as may be, but let's be honest, you have unusually small feet for a man. That's what makes it unique. Besides, if the footprint isn't yours why would anyone go to the trouble of destroying it?"

For a moment Lord Lowton appeared genuinely confused.

"We went back to look at the print again yesterday afternoon, to check it against the shoe in question, but when we got there, someone had deliberately dragged their heel across it. That sounds to me like something only a guilty man would do."

"Take no notice of her." Lord Beaufort put a hand on Lord Lowton's arm. "She hasn't got a hope of proving a footprint that no longer exists links you to the murder of Sir Cyril."

"All right then." Eliza took a deep breath and sat up to her full height. "Can you tell me how the murder weapon got into your boot room?"

"Murder weapon? I've no idea what you're talking about?"

"Oh, I think you do. The croquet mallet used to kill your brother, it's in your boot room."

Lord Lowton let out a sarcastic laugh. "That's where they live. We keep them down there so it's more convenient to pick them up when you go for a game."

"In that case, why was there only one in there, hidden in a corner? It didn't look like a convenient place to leave it. Nobody would have found it and besides, not everyone at the house keeps their shoes in the boot room."

"Maybe only five people played last time there was a game ... and Soams would have got the mallets for them."

"Or perhaps you didn't want us to find that particular one. There's no doubt it's the murder weapon, it still has traces of blood on the head around a small splinter."

"Well, it was nothing to do with me. Somebody's obviously trying to frame me."

"Well, if it wasn't you, who else could it be? Unless..." Eliza bit down on her lip as she glanced around the table. "There is one other person who has a small shoe size and access to the boot room ... your son. If you didn't murder your brother, are you lying to save Lord Albert?"

"No!" Caroline jumped to her feet. "How can you even think such a thing?"

Eliza rounded on her friend. "Because he was on the scene before anyone else and we know he'd arranged to meet someone there."

"He's been with Henry all week." Lady Caroline's voice pierced the room as she glared at Henry. "He could just as easily have killed Cyril and tried to frame Neville. Given his infatuation with Lady Alice, he'd have a motive on both counts."

"Don't bring me into it." Henry had watched the exchange with his eyes wide, but now he sank back into his chair. "I wasn't even there, I was by the library waiting for Lord Albert."

"A fine alibi that is if you were on your own," Lord Beaufort said.

Eliza's eyes narrowed. "He wasn't on his own. He was with Lady Alice as he told you."

"Alice? She told me she'd gone for a lie-down ahead of the ball," Lady Caroline said.

"Probably to get out of the way of everyone who wants to run her life for her," Henry said.

"That's a preposterous thing to say. We want what's best for her."

"Well, you've got a funny way of showing it."

Lord Albert entered the room unnoticed until he approached the table. "Sorry I'm late, what's all the shouting about?"

Eliza gazed at the young man before turning to Lord Lowton. "Perhaps we should ask him what he knows."

Lord Lowton's face turned a deep red. "He knows nothing, leave him out of this."

"I will if you tell me the truth."

"Stop one moment." Lord Albert held up his hand. "What don't I know?"

Eliza dabbed her napkin against her mouth and stood up. "Lord Albert, you were down by the lake on the morning your uncle was murdered, could you tell me...?"

Lord Beaufort slammed his hand onto the table. "Lord Lowton has just told you he knows nothing and I will not have you pursuing this nonsense. I have found your father guilty of the murder of Sir Cyril and the police are transferring him to London later today where he will be charged. His trial will follow shortly after. With all the trouble you've caused this family, I'll personally see to it that he hangs."

"You can't do that." Connie's voice sounded timid as she stood by Eliza's side. "Eliza's only been doing what any good investigator would do, not just taking the easy option like you did."

"I can and I will. Now I believe His Lordship told you to go ... be off with you."

"I've told you, we will, but not before you tell us what's going on here." Eliza rested both hands on the table as she leaned forward. "Both you and Lord Lowton lied about your whereabouts last Saturday morning, in the case of Lord Lowton, twice, and I want to know why."

"Out now." Lord Lowton marched around the table to

grab Eliza's arm but she was too quick for him and moved to the far side of the table.

"Inspector Adams had an appointment with the chief constable this morning and was hoping to file a report about you." Eliza's voice squeaked as she spoke. "I expect they'll be here shortly."

Lord Beaufort turned in his chair and laughed. "You don't think the police will do anything, do you? I've already spoken to the chief constable and I could have Inspector Adams out of New Scotland Yard before the end of the day if I wanted to."

"So you're trying to corrupt the police to save yourselves?"

"Don't be so surprised." Lord Beaufort gave her a withering glare. "The police know who to look after, and it isn't the likes of you."

Eliza glowered at the man in disgust, not able to find the right words.

"I'm afraid you've picked the wrong person this time." Connie walked around the table and took hold of Eliza's arm. "We've a friend whose son works on Fleet Street. She owes Eliza a favour and I'm sure we could get a detailed story in the newspaper before it goes to court."

"Y-yes." Eliza nodded at Connie. "Yes, we could ... and we will if we have to. Is that what you want or are you going to save yourselves the humiliation and tell us what happened?"

CHAPTER TWENTY-SIX

A chill ran down Eliza's spine and she shivered as Lord Lowton stepped towards her. Instinctively, she backed away before her resolve returned. Straightening her shoulders she looked him in the eye.

"Let me tell you what I think happened."

Lord Lowton stopped where he was. "You've no idea what went on."

Ignoring him, Eliza continued. "I believe that either you struck the blow that killed your brother ... or Lord Albert did and you're covering up for him."

"I didn't do it." Lord Albert's shriek filled the room, drawing everyone's attention. "It was Uncle Cyril who had the croquet mallet."

"Be quiet, Albert." Lord Lowton glowered at his son.

"But it wasn't me. I'm going back to Cambridge on Saturday and I'm not going as an accused murderer."

"I said be quiet."

"It was you who told me to lie."

Eliza stared at Lord Lowton. "What did you tell him to lie about?"

"He didn't lie." Lord Lowton pulled himself up to his full five feet six inches tall. "He was in the garden walking around the lake like he said."

"But that's the first time we've heard about Sir Cyril with the mallet. Did you and he argue ... again?"

"We hadn't argued."

"There you go again." Eliza's nostrils flared as she glared at the man not six feet away from her. "Are you incapable of telling the truth? We already know you argued on Saturday morning about the quality of the guests coming to the ball, myself and Mrs Appleton included. Was Sir Cyril still upset when you met him by the lake?"

"It wasn't like that."

"Well, what was it like? I think we can safely say Sir Cyril didn't hit himself over the back of the head with a mallet."

"He was trying to kill me!" Lord Albert's voice cut across Eliza and she paused as her gaze travelled around the room, her mind churning.

"Sir Cyril wanted to kill Lord Albert? Why would he do that?" Her gaze rested on Lord Lowton.

"Because Albert was the only person stopping Cyril from inheriting the title and estate when I die. With Albert out of the way, Cyril and David would have it all."

Eliza put her fingers to her forehead as she studied Lord Albert. "It was Sir Cyril who asked you to meet him at the lake, wasn't it? Is that who you were waiting for when Lady Victoria and Lord David left you?"

Lord Albert finally took a seat next to Henry. "He said he

wanted to talk to me but I wasn't to tell anyone. I didn't see him arrive ... I was looking out over the lake ... but suddenly I heard a noise behind me. When I turned, Uncle Cyril was standing behind me with the mallet raised like a golf club."

"And so you wrestled it from him and hit him on the back of the head before pushing him into the water?"

Eliza thought Lord Albert was about to cry.

"No, it wasn't like that. Father, tell them."

"So it *was* you." Eliza turned on her heel to face Lord Lowton. "You grabbed the mallet and hit your brother? We always knew the angle of the swing had come from a man shorter than Sir Cyril."

"Can't you see it was self-defence?" Lord Lowton yelled. "I'd overheard Cyril asking to speak to Albert and so I made my way to the lake. When I saw Cyril with the mallet raised above Albert's head I panicked and made a grab for it. I wanted to take it from him so we could talk, but he turned on me ... his eyes were wild ... the only way I could stop him from hurting either myself or Albert was to use the mallet on him. I didn't mean to hit him so hard, but when he fell into the water I panicked."

"And so you disappeared into your ditch rather quickly leaving my father to find the body and take the blame."

"It wasn't meant to happen," Lord Lowton said. "If Cyril hadn't..."

"Forget Sir Cyril." Eliza's voice was venomous. "If you'd owned up to what you did, my father wouldn't have spent the last week in a police cell." She glared at Lord Beaufort. "How much of this did you know?"

"Nothing..." He squirmed in his seat as Eliza's eyes remained fixed on him. "Not immediately anyway. His

Lordship asked me to provide him with an alibi and so I did. He didn't tell me why."

"I've a good mind to report you for interfering with the administration of justice..."

A smirk crossed Lord Beaufort's face as he pushed himself up from the table. "You needn't think we'll let you walk out of here and report all this."

The blood drained from Eliza's face as she and Connie both stepped backwards and glanced towards the door.

"I wouldn't bother trying to escape," Lord Lowton said. "Soams will have heard everything and won't let you out. You should have left when I told you to, now you'll have to stay. We can take a walk in the garden after luncheon ..."

Connie bolted towards the door, just as it opened.

"There's no need for any more threats, sir." Inspector Adams led a group of men into the room and signalled to two uniformed officers to put handcuffs on both Lords Lowton and Beaufort.

"Lord Lowton, I'm arresting you for the murder of the Honourable Cyril Lowton. Lord Beaufort, I'm arresting you for interfering with the administration of justice."

"Get out immediately." Lord Lowton punched the officer wrestling with the handcuffs as he struggled to break free. "How did you get in here? SOAMS!"

Two further constables hurried to help their colleagues.

"I think I'm right in saying it's your butler's afternoon off," Inspector Adams said. "A maid let us in."

"Damn that man." Lord Lowton continued to struggle until the officers held him against the wall, his hands cuffed behind his back.

"We've been standing outside since Lord Albert joined

you and I must say, Mrs Thomson's done an excellent job of getting you to tell her what's been going on."

"None of it was true." Lord Beaufort tried to squeeze his hands from the cuffs. "We were only telling her what she wanted to hear."

"That will be for the courts to decide." A man who had stood to the back of the group stepped forward and Eliza smiled as she noticed Archie standing beside him.

"Chief Constable." Lord Beaufort froze. "What are you doing here? You told me this case would be closed."

"And so it was for about a quarter of an hour. Unfortunately, I was left with no choice but to reopen it. Inspector Adams told me of the goings-on this week, but after our conversation the other day, naturally I didn't believe him and told him to close the case immediately."

"So what changed your mind, man? I told you the case against Bell was watertight."

The chief constable strolled into the centre of the room. "Dr Thomson here." He beckoned Archie to step forward. "Inspector Adams was leaving my office when Dr Thomson arrived, insisting he speak to me in person."

Eliza shuddered as Lord Lowton glared at her husband.

"You! After everything I did for you last weekend."

"Offering a couple of days of hospitality excuses no one of murder, Neville, you should know that," the chief constable said. "What I hadn't realised was precisely who Mr Bell is."

"What's that got to do with it?" Lord Lowton said.

"It's got everything to do with it. You told me the murderer was a lowlife who had outstayed his welcome after the ball. That's not true, is it? Dr Thomson pointed out that

Mr Bell is, in fact, a very respected member of society who deserves a fair hearing. He brought with him the report from the coroner that confirmed all that Adams had told me. He also told me of the whitewash that was your inquiry. You pressed no one about their alibis or confirmed they were true. From the beginning, the only person in your sights was poor Mr Bell."

Lord Lowton shook his arm from the hold of a constable and walked to the chief constable. "If you've been listening to this conversation, you'll know that the death of my brother was in self-defence. You can't arrest us for that."

"And you can't try to put the blame on an innocent man."

"Well, he shouldn't have been interfering." He nodded towards Eliza. "If that daughter of his hadn't insisted it was murder, we could have recorded it as accidental drowning and nobody would have been any the wiser."

"That's a terrible thing to say." Eliza couldn't hold her tongue any longer.

"No, it's not. My brother was about to murder my son and he got what was coming to him."

"And are his wife and children happy about that?"

Lord Lowton stopped and stared at Eliza. "Victoria? What's it got to do with her?"

"You tell us. You were with her for long enough last night."

Eliza saw Lady Caroline's mouth drop open but Inspector Adams filled the silence.

"We've sent officers to arrest Lady Victoria and Colonel Hawkins as accomplices to the cover-up. We also have men waiting for Soams when he returns. Lord and Lady Forsyth will be taken in for questioning and for withholding

evidence." He turned to the uniformed officers. "Take Their Lordships away."

"You won't get away with this," Lord Beaufort said as a constable led him to the door. "I'll see you out of a job before the end of this."

Whether Lord Beaufort was talking to Inspector Adams or the chief constable Eliza didn't know, but a moment later, she failed to care when the door to the dining room opened and a police officer ushered in Mr Bell.

"Father!" She hurried to his side and took his arm.

"Ah, Mr Bell," the chief constable said. "I'm glad you could join us."

Mr Bell grimaced. "Not as glad as I am, but that's only because my previous residence was rather short of space. They've owned up, have they?"

Inspector Adams smiled. "Thanks to your daughter here."

Eliza smiled. "I can't take all the credit. It seems you wouldn't have been here to hear the confession had it not been for Archie."

"Archie?" Mr Bell raised an eyebrow at her husband.

"Yes, sir," the chief constable said. "Unfortunately Lord Beaufort had me fooled, and it was only the appearance of Dr Thomson that persuaded me to relook at the evidence."

Mr Bell extended his hand to his son-in-law. "It seems I owe you an apology ... Archie. Thank you."

CHAPTER TWENTY-SEVEN

E liza sat back in her chair and pushed her empty plate away. The dining room of her father's house may not be as grand as the one in Lowton Hall, but it was so much more comfortable.

"That was delicious." She turned to her left and smiled at Mr Bell. "Sunday luncheon with my whole family and without feeling a lump in my stomach as I was eating it."

"At least you've been properly fed this week," Mr Bell said. "I've had to make do with bread and water."

"I don't know how you managed," Henry said as he finished off his second helping of roast beef.

"Unfortunately, you don't get a lot of choice in the matter."

"Well, I think it's most unfair," Connie said. "They should give you decent meals, at least until they find you guilty."

"My dear, they thought I was guilty. Lord Beaufort set me up like a fool and they nearly fell for it."

The maid came in to clear the plates as Mr Bell stood up

and walked to the sideboard. "Archie, may I get you a drink? A brandy perhaps."

Archie smiled at his father-in-law. "Yes, I'd like that, thank you."

"Ladies. A small glass of port? After all, we are celebrating."

With the drinks poured, and Henry's glass of ale refilled, Mr Bell proposed a toast. "To the best family and friends a man could have, thank you all."

"And to Mr Bell. May he never again be incarcerated," Archie said.

"I'll second that." Mr Bell raised his glass to Archie.

The sound of the doorbell interrupted the clink of glasses.

"Who on earth's calling at this time on a Sunday?" Mr Bell stepped into the hallway as the maid answered the door. "Inspector Adams, what are you doing here? Come on in, man, as long as you've not come to arrest me again."

"As if I would." Inspector Adams followed him into the dining room. "I was passing and wanted to give you an update on what's been going on since you left Lowton Hall. I had a feeling Dr and Mrs Thomson may still be here."

"Well, come and take a seat then. May I get you a brandy?"

Inspector Adams eyed the glasses around the table. "I shouldn't, but just a small one, to wet my whistle, you understand."

Mr Bell poured a small measure and passed it to the inspector before retaking his seat.

"So what news do you have for us?" Archie asked. "Has anyone been charged?"

"Not yet, but they will be. Lord Beaufort is trying everything possible to claim their innocence, but it looks like he'll be stripped of his knighthood at the very least."

"It couldn't happen to a nicer man." Eliza frowned as she took a sip of her drink.

"But will the charges stick?" Mr Bell said.

"I hope so. Lord Lowton's expected to be charged with manslaughter rather than murder given that the death wasn't premeditated but having said that, given his status, he may escape jail. Lord Beaufort may not be so lucky. For a man in his position to abuse his office so seriously, we hope he'll serve time. They're both out on bail at the moment though, which makes me uneasy."

"Will you charge Lord Albert with anything?" Henry asked.

"It's not looking likely. In theory he could be charged with interfering with the administration of justice but I doubt he will be. He's a minor who was told what to do and say by two powerful men, so he'll likely escape with a reprimand."

Henry smiled. "So he'll be back at Cambridge."

"I can live with that," Mr Bell said. "I don't believe any of my misfortune was down to him."

"No, you're right, and now we've learned the truth about what happened from the other guests who were at the house, it appears that Sir Cyril was the master of his own downfall."

"Was it his anger about bringing commoners into the family that caused it?" Eliza asked.

"I'd say that was the basis of it. We know he'd resented Lady Caroline for over twenty years because she was a commoner, but apparently the day before the ball, he'd found

235

out that Lady Victoria was having a liaison with Colonel Hawkins."

"You owe me an apology, Mother." Henry grinned as Eliza glowered at him.

The inspector glanced between the two of them before continuing. "As you can imagine, he was furious, but she refused to be intimidated by a petulant husband, which only made things worse."

"Could that be why he was in such a bad mood with Lord Lowton?" Connie asked.

"It won't have helped, but there was something else. I think you know that Lord Albert had told his father on the Friday that he'd met a girl at Cambridge that he wanted to marry. Well, Lady Hilda finally admitted that Sir Cyril had confided to her that he had overheard the conversation. He expected her to share his indignation, but when she didn't, he exploded and challenged Lord Lowton about it."

"That would explain why he was in such a bad mood with Henry on the Friday evening as well." Eliza looked again at her son. "When he saw you sitting with Lady Alice, he must have envisioned the whole family descending into the middle classes."

"So that was enough to make him think it would be a good idea to murder Lord Albert?" Connie asked.

"So it would seem," Inspector Adams said.

"I've just remembered something," Eliza said. "When we found out Lady Victoria had been into the garden to fetch Lord David, she said it was because Sir Cyril was angry that their son was with Lord Albert when he had reading to do. She wasn't concerned because he wasn't due back at school for another week, but she said ... now, what was it?

Something like 'When Cyril's in one of his moods it's best not to argue.'"

Inspector Adams studied her. "So, are you suggesting that Sir Cyril had made arrangements to meet Lord Albert, but when he heard his son might be present, he had to find a reason to get rid of him?"

"That's what it sounds like."

Inspector Adams made a note in his ever-present notebook. "I don't suppose it will make any difference to the proceedings, but I suppose it confirms that Sir Cyril has no one to blame but himself."

"What's Lady Victoria had to say about it all? Was she involved?" Eliza asked.

"No, we don't think so, other than by upsetting Sir Cyril, although Lady Hilda also let slip that everyone knew Lady Victoria and Lord Lowton had 'an arrangement' ... well, everyone except Lady Caroline. Apparently, among the ruling classes it's not uncommon and even Sir Cyril wasn't too upset by it. They all thought Lady Caroline wouldn't understand though and so they never spoke of it."

"She's a right one, isn't she, that Lady Victoria?" Connie sat up straight before emptying her glass of port. "How could she be so brazen?"

Henry sat with a wide grin on his face as he watched Connie.

"Is that why Lord Lowton went to see her the other night?" Eliza asked.

"So it would seem. He may be more open-minded than his brother but he still had concerns that she was fraternising with a hired hand and apparently told her that unless she stopped, she would have to leave the estate. Unfortunately for her, Lord Lowton had rather more clout than his brother."

"Why didn't he just get rid of the colonel?" Connie asked.

Inspector Adams shrugged. "Who knows? We confirmed that Lord Lowton did pay him to provide an alibi and to keep an eye on you when you were down by the lake. My guess is that he wanted to keep him close rather than sending him back to London with all the opportunities for gossip that would entail."

"So no one else is being charged with interfering with the administration of justice?" Archie asked as Mr Bell stood up to refill the glasses.

"Not as many as I'd like. We've no evidence that Lady Victoria was part of the conspiracy and the Forsyths have their own legal counsel who says his clients knew nothing of it. He's representing the colonel, as well, and will probably get him acquitted. The only other person we may be able to nail is Soams. Apparently, he had a habit of standing outside doors listening to what was going on and so he would have known exactly what Lord Lowton and Lord Beaufort were up to. He probably listened in on some of your private conversations too. We hope to charge him with withholding information."

"So that's it then?" Mr Bell said. "I had a letter from Sir Rodney yesterday morning to say that Caroline will stay at Lowton Hall for the time being and will run the house if His Lordship ends up in jail." He laughed. "I'm sure Sir Cyril would be furious. The one thing he was trying to stop is the thing most likely to happen. Oh, the irony!"

THANK YOU FOR READING!

I hope you enjoyed the book. If you did, I'd really appreciate it if you could leave a review.

As well as making me happy, reviews help the book gain visibility and can bring it to the attention of more readers who may enjoy it.

To leave a review, visit your local Amazon store and type VL McBeath into the search bar.

This should bring up my author page where you will see *Death of an Honourable Gent*.

Click on the book and scroll down to the review section of the page and click on "Write a Customer Review".

My only plea. Please no spoilers!

Thank You!

AUTHOR'S NOTES AND ACKNOWLDGEMENTS

Until now, all of my books have focussed on the lives of either the poor working classes or the well-to-do middle classes. While I've enjoyed writing each one, I've secretly been envious of those who write about the glamorous lifestyles of the aristocracy, particularly as it was in its heyday in pre-war England.

Given that Eliza's father had become rather wealthy thanks to the opportunities offered by the industrial revolution, I thought he and the family would be suitably well connected to warrant an invitation to a stately home for the weekend.

By the time I was editing the book, however, all those titles where driving me mad!

How did each character address their peers? Should a title be dropped because the characters were on intimate terms? Would the title still be used if these characters where talking about their spouse or child to a third party...? The list went on.

Fortunately, thanks to my wonderful editor Susan, I think we got there in the end.

As always, I must thank my family and friends for reading various drafts of the book and giving me feedback. I couldn't have done it without them.

Finally, I'd like to thank you for reading. I hope to see you for the next book!

ALSO BY VL MCBEATH

Eliza Thomson Investigates:

A Deadly Tonic (A Novella)

Murder in Moreton

Dying for a Garden Party

Look out for the newsletter that will include details of launch dates and special offers for future books in the series.

To sign up visit: https://www.subscribepage.com/ETI_SignUp

∿

The *Ambition & Destiny* Series

Based on a true story of one family's trials, tribulations and triumphs as they seek their fortune in Victorian-era England.

Short Story Prequel: *Condemned by Fate*

(available as a FREE download when you get Part 1)

Part 1: *Hooks & Eyes*

Part 2: *Less Than Equals*

Part 3: *When Time Runs Out*

Part 4: *Only One Winner*

Part 5: *Different World*

For further details, search 'VL McBeath Amazon Author Page'

Made in United States
North Haven, CT
05 November 2021